# *Dear Mr Kawabata*
## RASHID AL-DAIF

**Translated by Paul Starkey**
**Foreword by Margaret Drabble**

**Quartet Books**

This book has been translated and published with the assistance of the European Cultural Foundation within the framework of a programme launched simultaneously by editors in different European languages. Each of the retraced journeys in this series offers to European readers some Arab aspects of a shared heritage, the 'Mémoires de la Méditerranée'.

The programme currently includes the following languages: Catalan, Dutch, English, French, German, Italian, Polish, Spanish and Swedish.

First published in Great Britain by Quartet Books Limited 1999
A member of the Namara Group
27 Goodge Street
London W1P 2LD

Copyright © by Rashid al-Daif 1995
Translation copyright © by Paul Starkey 1999

A catalogue record for this book is available from the British Library

ISBN 0 7043 8113 3

Phototypeset by FSH Ltd
Printed and bound in Great Britain by Cox & Wyman, Reading, Berks

To Shafiq

# Foreword

*Dear Mr Kawabata* is a haunting, disturbing, gripping story from the heart of the Lebanese civil war. Rashid al-Daif, who was born in 1945 into a Christian Maronite family in a Lebanese village, lived through the experiences he describes, but this is not a simple auto-biographical account of suffering, martyrdom or heroism. It is an interrogation of history, full of ambiguities: it takes on broad themes of national consciousness, patriotism, and revolutionary politics, and explores them with poetic insight and painful honesty. Its format is that of an extended letter to the Japanese novelist Yasunari Kawabata, who committed suicide in 1972 at the age of seventy-three, having been awarded the Nobel Prize in 1968: al-Daif himself, as we learn from this narration, had himself been near to death, and his questions to his distinguished dead colleague reverberate through a long repeating un-answered litany of appeal.

This is an international novel-memoir, in which the implications of local events grow outwards from a traditional village childhood, described here with great tenderness: we meet mother, father, aunt, neighbours, school friends, schoolmasters, and we taste the milk of the goat and the olive bread. But we emerge into a global panorama, and into events that dominated our voyeuristic television screens in the West for more than a decade. (Did Mr Kawabata in Japan know of the Lebanese conflict and the issues of Palestinian nationalism? What did any of us know of them? These are some of the questions posed.) The story moves (though, importantly, with a circular rather than a linear movement) from a schoolboy's sense of metaphysical shock as he learns that the world spins on its axis, through his intellectual, sexual and political education, to a bloody dénouement. This is a classic account of an idealistic young man's awakening, his confrontation with patriarchy and ignorance, his espousing of radical politics, his involvement with armed conflict, and his mature mid-life re-assessment of himself and the country where he still lives and works. I do not know how much of it is fact, how much fiction, for this is neither a novel nor a confession. But every word of it rings true.

It is also a work of art. Rashid al-Daif is a poet as well as a novelist, and he uses language with elegant precision, and with his own insistent questioning of the possibilities of translation. This is not a florid or rhetorical work: if anything it tends towards minimalism and the surreal objectivity and understatement of the *nouveau roman*. It convinces. It enlarges our understanding, and deserves to take its place with other memorable accounts of the courage and complexities of civil war, such as Orwell's *Homage to Catalonia*. Both Orwell and al-Daif were wounded in the neck: neither of them was silenced. Their testimony lives on.

I met Rashid many years ago when he was still a student: he was the first to present me in person with the dilemma of the radical Lebanese, and I remember long discussions of Israel, of Palestine, and of Arab perceptions of America. These were an education to me. I have read some of his work in French, and it is good to be able to welcome this fine English-language translation of *Dear Mr Kawabata*, a strange and wholly original work. This writer speaks from a world of which we need to know more, but his work is not, to quote one of his own more trenchant observations of West–East perception, a work of 'Exotica'. It is too shrewd and subtle for that. Rashid al-Daif is not a man for nationalistic simplicities. His voice is human, and his own.

Margaret Drabble
March, 1999

I was walking along Hamra Street in Beirut when I suddenly saw him, and for a moment I thought that I was seeing myself. At first I thought that I was merely seeing someone who resembled me closely, but I quickly realized that there was more to it than mere resemblance. 'I must be in front of a shop window or mirror,' I said to myself, 'that is reflecting an uncannily sharp image of myself.' But the reflection was walking in a different direction, with a different gait, wearing different clothes. This was not my reflection, then, but myself. I was seeing myself.

*Perhaps this never happened to you, Mr Kawabata. It's an uncommon thing. But it does happen, and it happened to me. And why should it be strange for something to happen only occasionally? Aren't things that happen occasionally part of our daily lives? I'm certain that you — unlike most other people — don't see anything disconcerting about things happening only occasionally. In fact, that is why I have chosen you.*

For a moment I thought that I was seeing myself walking along the opposite pavement just a few metres away. The moment, however, seemed to become longer, increasing not just my surprise but also my feeling of emptiness. I was almost losing my balance — losing the sense of cohesion that held the parts of my body together and joined them to that mysterious something that controlled my entire being.

For a moment — a moment which was growing longer and longer — I thought that I was disintegrating and that each part of me was going in a different direction. I went weak at the knees and almost collapsed to the ground before I could pull myself together.

It is said, Mr Kawabata, that at the moment when a man dies, his whole life flashes before his eyes like a film and he recalls everything that has happened to him from his birth to his last moment. I can assure you that nothing like this happened to me. When I died several times in the moments after I had been wounded in the neck and shoulder, in every part of my body, I did not remember anything at all. No memories of any sort whatever passed in front of my eyes. Nothing, not even the world after death, could distract me from the pain I was feeling. My pain was the only thing to occupy my senses when I returned to life from the vastness of death.

It is also said, Mr Kawabata, that it is only the drowning man who sees the film of his life flashing past his eyes like that. I have never died from drowning and to this day, so far as I know, nobody has been able to prove the truth of this assertion. Or disprove it either.

I did see the film of my life flashing past me, however, swiftly but clearly, with my own eyes. It was a moment that was quickly over, but it has imprinted itself on my memory. It happened when I met him (the above-mentioned person) in Hamra Street, and for a moment thought I was seeing myself.

*I say 'met him', and 'the above-mentioned person', Mr Kawabata, rather than naming him explicitly, because among us, people do not mention the names of their enemies when speaking about them. Instead, we allude to them with an adjective, pronoun, circumlocution, gesture or silence.*

I saw him walking along the Hamra Street pavement as if nothing had happened. It was as if the horrors that had taken place all over Lebanon, and in Beirut in particular, for the last fifteen years were an artificial flood, specially constructed for a short-term purpose — an open-air play, perhaps, or to shoot a film. The hair on my head stood on end and my blood began to boil.

*I hate him, Mr Kawabata.*

He was walking along with his head tilted slightly back

in an arrogant pose, holding a *misbaha*\* in both hands level with the top of his stomach. *Naturally, unlike other people, Japanese or not, you know what a* misbaha *is. I was once in Paris with a* misbaha *in my hand, and one of my French friends asked me whether it was a pastime. 'Yes!' I answered. 'For us Arabs, time does not pass without a* misbaha*!'*

His bearing was upright, despite a slight paunch.

He was looking into the distance on a pavement swarming with people – passers-by, street-sellers, militiamen, all sorts of people, some just waiting there.

Who else could walk along like this, so bashfully and precisely, on the Hamra Street pavement in Beirut in 1991, when the war had scarcely yet shed its burdens? *Notice this expression, Mr Kawabata – 'the war had shed its burdens'; you will see how many similar expressions of eternal beauty we have in Arabic.* The pavement was riddled with cracks and holes that would have taken a man down to the bottom of hell if he had fallen into them.

Except for the man who I thought was myself, nobody else would have been capable of it!

His authentic, Semitic nose was raised a little, arrogantly, like his head.

The sight of him angered me intolerably. *There are no really new feelings; every feeling is fixed forever in the depths of a man's heart.* I said: 'It is impossible that I should ever have been his friend, kept him company almost every day for years, and fought with him. I must have just invented him!'

I had invented him!

I had assembled his component parts from similar features common to many other people I know, features which also link them with myself. I had pulled them together to make him!

---

\* Worry beads

3

He did not see me.

Not because I was not in his field of vision, but because he only saw people he wanted to see, and he did not want to see me!

He only wanted to see people who had deserved his favour. And I did not deserve his favour.

He was three centimetres taller than me, but that did not give him the right to look down on me. A lot of other people are taller than me, and a lot are shorter. What has this got to do with anything? And again, since when has height been a measure of value, and a reason to feel superior?

I tell you, Mr Kawabata, that it was really I who made him three centimetres taller than me, or more, or however much he wanted. I had no hesitation or diffidence about that. I would do it for him, and anything else he wanted, with complete self-confidence, and with no reservations of any kind.

What really annoyed me, Mr Kawabata, was something else, something else a few metres, miles, or generations away from me.

I will draw your attention in advance, Mr Kawabata, to the fact that I may appear to switch from one subject to another while I am speaking. But I am confident that you will quickly understand the underlying reason behind each switch. The style will actually be an object of admiration on your part, as well as a reason for happiness on my part, because I will find in you a rare Arab, who will surrender to me out of love for the days to come and the places to come.

I do not describe you as an Arab, Mr Kawabata, by way of paradox. I do not like paradoxes, and I consider those who like them to be lacking in culture and intelligence.

4

When I mention the days to come, I am not referring to the future. For you, there are no days yet to come. You know that better than anyone. But my days are in me, they are mine, I mean . . .

What do I mean?

I do not mean anything, I am being carried away by words. How many people like me have been carried away by words – other people, other generations!

The same words with which we – you will find out later the reason for my using the plural form – believed we could take the world in our hands.

Then it became clear to me – notice that I have returned to the singular form – that we were good at dealing with them, but not with the world.

We rode the words – *you are no doubt thinking of a horse, but in Arabic the verb is used of riding a camel* – and raced them wherever we wanted.

Wherever we wanted!

We moved with the speed of lightning from 'surplus value' to 'the historical role' of the working class in manufacturing this surplus, to 'the objective necessity' of participating in the war – I mean the Lebanese war. *I believe that this specification is timely, since the word 'war' can certainly be ambiguous, if its place and time are not defined; you yourself might wrongly think of one of the Japanese wars, for example.*

With the speed of lightning! *Notice this eternally beautiful expression!*

We were good at overcoming obstacles and hurdles. We were horsemen. Our tongues were extraordinarily agile.

*I did not yet know, Mr Kawabata, that every time the earth rotates, it produces more casualties!*

We took words for our mounts, confident that we were riding history!

We grasped the reins of history and raced it towards the goal it had defined for itself: Communism, by way of Socialism.

Our role was to steer events in the right direction, to remove the obstacles from the path of history's wheel – *notice this expression* – so that it should not be held up or get stuck.

History could not go forward without our daily intervention. We were its makers, and at the same time we were part of it. *We liked to bring together contradictions in a single linguistic formula, so that language would be a true, faithful, scientific reflection of a reality based on contradiction: the unity of contradictions in objective reality expressed itself in a linguistic reality – or even in a single phrase.*

*I wonder in all sincerity, Mr Kawabata, what is wrong with saying this?*

The world, with all its constituent parts, was simply words turned into things. As soon as the word changed, the thing would change: water, earth, air, individuals, groups – in short, all living and inanimate creatures.

All that was required was that the masses should learn these word-truths, and perfect their use, for the course of history to be changed. This was our mission.

The ruling class realized this, and realized in particular that it was against its interest. Its interest was to hide the truth, because the truth liberates. *Amen!*

. . . until one day, at the beginning of the war – *our war* – in 1975, I realized that my mouth was full of ants, that my lips were stitched together like a deep wound sewn up with strong thread. A sort of dream began to dog me, a dream that a huge half-statue was lurking in the midst of a desert that extended to infinity in every direction, spread out like a sea smooth as oil, under a sky that was cloudy and endless, merging with the limitless desert at the farthest horizon. Everything was calm and quiet. Not a whisper of a breeze, not a sound. Not a tree, not a blade of grass. Not a bird, not an animal. Only this enormous half-statue in the middle of the desert, under the vault of the cloud-filled sky. Suddenly soldiers emerged from the two ears of the statue, small as one's little finger, carrying machine-guns, which they let off in all directions, firing on everything indiscriminately. It was as if everything in this environment was hostile to them. Then they hurried down the folds of the statue until they reached the sandy ground, wet from the rain that had stopped only a few moments ago. They went off into the desert in every direction – so many of them that they could not be counted; it was as if they themselves had turned into the sand. Then they disappeared into the infinite expanse.

Their bullets made no sound.

This dream stayed with me, together with the feeling of ants crawling inside a mouth I could not open. A certain conviction was born inside me. The war was still in the first stages of its fury, which meant that only madness could speak of this reality, for it defied all normal expression. *I was still insisting on speaking of reality.*

*I ask myself in all sincerity, Mr Kawabata, whether I have changed, and how, and whether for the better!*

I tried to express my conviction by saying: 'Night is truth, and day is clarification.'

*You did not know that I write these sorts of expression, which I mean as a summary of complex, urgent situations, urgent and articulate.*

*A summary, I mean them as a summary.*

Dear Mr Kawabata,

I always used to dream of being appointed king of some distant peoples. I would rule over them with justice, and dedicate myself to their service.

I dreamed that I would be appointed as an arbitrator between warring factions, in some part of the world, to provide a model of fair play.

I dreamed that my father would take me with him to the city to see faces which I could not see in the village. The night I went with him to Beirut Airport for the first time, I was so agitated that I could not sleep. I spent the night imagining my happiness when I saw so many types and sorts of people.

I dreamed that I could speak every language perfectly, so that I could eavesdrop on everyone!

I loved the innocence of the stranger. Perhaps I still do. The stranger's lack of preconceptions to me meant neutrality. Perhaps it still does.

So here I am, Mr Kawabata, appointing you as the king I dreamed of being myself, the arbitrator obeyed because of his sincerity.

Here I am taking your hand, to show you every corner of my country.

Above all, I liked your name as it sounded to us Arabs. Its sounds in our language are gentle, flowing and uncomplicated. They give an impression of familiarity. Also . . . aren't you the writer who wrote *The Master of Gō*, which wrung my heart, so great was my sympathy with the old teacher. I liked to see in his way of playing the wisdom of Japan and its noble (I mean, its ancient) history. This was in spite of my convictions, which were at odds with what I considered his intellectual position as reflected in his method of playing.

I also wanted, like you, to write a story in which I

would speak, through an ordinary event, about the clash between the climate of the age (I mean modernity, with its threats and challenges) and the local people, I mean tradition. This was despite my opposition to your way of constructing the story – though I certainly respect it.

Dear Mr Kawabata,

In so far as I, Rashid, am personally both the narrator and the subject of the story, allow me to make an observation, which I will certainly not direct to you (since you are already aware of it) but to other potential readers of this letter: I, the Rashid who am addressing Mr Kawabata, am not exactly Rashid the author. What links me to the author is the fact that he created me.

I admit that I am largely subject to his control.

However. . .

However, this subjection is not total, but partial or relative. And because it is only partial or relative, I am quite different from him.

For example, take the letters of the Arabic alphabet. Is there anything smaller than the difference between a *jim** and a *hā'***? It is just a dot! But this same dot makes the *jim* represent a sound totally different from the *hā'*, and turns *rahim* (the Merciful) into *rajim* (the cursed) when it is written!

Then again, even though I am the product of the writer's imagination, the writer is also a product of my separation from him, for I am his mirror. The influence is not one-way, but in both directions.

Anyone who wants to try the author for creating me has also to try me, for I am also his creator. Who will dare, then?

Who will dare to try me?

---

\* ج

\*\* ح

Who can do anything against the blue of the sky?

Kingdoms have fallen because they dared to try the author for the creature of his imagination – a creature that has wings to fly, and hovers like a phantom over the grave of his father seeking vengeance.

Mighty empires have fallen because they did not understand that the egg is not the chicken. The last of these empires was the Soviet Union – the dream of this century's dawn.

*I honestly wonder, Mr Kawabata, where is the sense in these words. I wonder whether it is possible for a man not to strive to give his tongue free rein.*

Mr Kawabata,

There is no doubt in my mind that the more I press on with what I have to say, the more eager you are to listen, despite the fact that your own style in constructing a narrative is to hurry to reach a conclusion, like a piece of architecture striving towards a perfect form. But your mind is open, no doubt, to other temperaments.

And again, you naturally listen to other people's problems and suffering.

Their suffering!

We Arabs find it natural to express our suffering, because we are peoples who have been oppressed and humiliated by time, which has appropriated everything we hold noble and sacred. *Like other peoples, Greeks, Portuguese, Turks, etc., etc.*

In so far as literature for us is a mirror of the age and of society, our literature (especially poetry) is pervaded by sadness, indeed sometimes by tears.

*Do you suppose that tears are what deprive our literature of the capacity to delve deeply into the secrets of its subjects? On*

*the basis that too much sadness deprives a man of the capacity*
*to see and understand clearly and intelligently, as the classical*
*Arabic dictionaries say?*

So far as I am concerned, I promise you straightaway
that I will not let you hear weeping, that I will not
complain, that I will not expose my suffering to you,
and that I will not grumble about the bad situation fate
has brought me to, as if I were a young prince reduced
by the world to an outcast. I will not rise up in revolt
against injustice and oppression, or complain to you of
the sufferings of this people, trampled under the foot of
reactionary regimes, the agents of colonialism, imperialism or the new Crusades.

No!

*What do I mean by 'no' here, Mr Kawabata?*

I promise you, and I will try to keep my promise.

I will try!

Now, Mr Kawabata, I hope that you will forget
everything else, and will pay attention only to what I am
going to say, because I shall go straight to the heart of
the matter – a matter that concerns you as much as it
concerns me. The last initiative that you took in your
life was simply the most eloquent proof of that. I say,
something inside me gives me pain, something metres,
miles or generations away!

I repeat, in case your mind was wandering at that
particular moment, something inside me gives me pain,
something metres, miles or generations away!

In saying this, I don't mean an organ in my body. The
state of my health is excellent. I wish that every man
could enjoy health as good.

Nor am I suffering from a psychological illness.

*You know what I am saying, no doubt, without the need for*

*all this explanation. It is simply a precaution, Mr Kawabata.*

My problem may be summed up, then, as knowing the time and place of my pain.

*I sense that you began to follow me from the very first moment. Didn't I tell you that the matter concerns you as much as it concerns me?*

Where and when, then, might this pain be? From which direction does it spring? From the past or from the future? Or from the two together, as they flow towards the present? *The past, Mr Kawabata, flows towards the present, and the future too. The present is both the future and the past of the whole of time.*

Talking about the future is a kind of prophecy, and I am the last person to be concerned with prophecies. On the other hand, I am certain that talking about the past is just as difficult as talking about the future. Don't you see, like me, the way different groups and sects in the country differ about events that have happened, about things that have been said, and about the blood that has flowed and is flowing and will continue to flow (*this is not a prophecy, but a conclusion based on a simple analogy.*

*Analogy!*)

concerning God's will for this world that he has created?

You are not to understand my words as diminishing the importance of historians and the science of history. Everyone has his function. But the earth rotates with us all, and every time it rotates, Mr Kawabata, its rotation produces casualties.

There is nothing left, therefore — you will agree with me about this — except memory, I mean my personal memory. My memory is a firm support for me, a support untouched by doubt.

I have a memory, Mr Kawabata, such that if I wished, I

could recollect the colour of every day I have lived from the moment I was born – or even earlier – until now.

It is a great blessing.

I remember. . . .

Winter was a passing stage of the year in our beautiful country when I was young. Then, as time went by and I grew older, it began to linger, until today it takes up almost half the year.

I remember. . .

The weather in our beautiful country was always warm and pleasant, and summer lasted the whole time.

Our house was security. The further I went away from it, the more cautious I became, for from faraway countries terrible news would reach us.

Temporary countries.

How could 'there' have hurt me at that time?

I remember. . .

Mr Kawabata, why is it that we, the ordinary people, or at least the ordinary élite, can only talk about the past with nostalgia? Why can't we simply talk about it in a neutral way? I would almost say objectively, but I hesitate to.

Or is it that the past, among all the moments of time, is the strongest – or even the only present?

I did not realize, Mr Kawabata, until I was older, that my father had not been present on the day our greatest hero returned secretly from exile. Indeed, he had not even been born yet, and his parents had not even married!

He would embark on the story as if he wanted to convince me that I was there too. Listen to how he used to tell it:

'After a long absence, one night while people were sleeping, Abu al-Badawi was woken up by the sound

13

of footsteps. He didn't believe what his ears were hearing. They were the Bey's footsteps, he knew them. He listened carefully, they were definitely his. He listened more carefully, they were coming closer, they were heading towards the door of the church. He went out barefoot and before he had spoken a single word to him pulled on the bellrope. Only a few moments later, the church square and the paths leading to it were crammed full of people.'

I was certain, Mr Kawabata, that my father saw the incident, until one day, quite by chance, I made a simple arithmetical calculation: the Bey had fled from his exile in Italy well before the end of the nineteenth century, while my father – so he mentioned once in front of me – was born just before the beginning of the First World War in 1914.

So he could not have been there.

Mr Kawabata, I know that people need dreams, fairy-tales, religions, or whatever... I know all that. But...

But a simple mathematical calculation proves that he wasn't there. It proves it! Listen. I remember...

She (forgive me for not revealing how close her relationship was to me) used to say to him in a whisper: 'Go away before the butchers get up.' She would call me to sleep beside her, before *he* stretched out on the other side, so that if a husband or relative or neighbour surprised her, I would be the excuse for anything – any movement or noise. She would entice me with presents. I had to sleep as soon as I had slipped into her bed. I didn't tell the secret to anyone except my sister, who was later married off to *his* son after patient negotiations.

Sure, sure, sure... these are very rare things, and departures from general upright conduct. But our direct ancestors, Mr Kawabata, and their descendants, spent their lives skulking at street-corners in the village, to assassinate each other in a hellish cycle of revenge.

The blood revenge never dried up. Especially when the political leadership was in charge of organizing and managing it.

Dear Mr Kawabata,

I am a Maronite (I mean that I was born into a Maronite family, and grew up in a Maronite environment). I love goat's yoghurt and long-lived mountain trees: cedars, junipers, pines, holm-oaks.

Sir,

This piece of information would be valueless if confined to a personal, individual taste. Many Muslims – Sunni and Shi'ite alike – love goat's yoghurt and mountain trees. Many Maronites, and Christians generally, find that goat's yoghurt and mountain trees mean nothing to them, and they have no preference for mountains over coast, sea or desert.

But symbols transcend the things they symbolize, and soar aloft on their own wings.

Goats are creatures of the rugged mountains, and it was in mountains like these that I was born and grew up. And the long-lived mountain trees, which stand firm in the face of storms, rain and snow, are a victory, even if only a temporary one, over time.

You have heard, no doubt, about the cedars of Lebanon which live for thousands of years. They grow there, high in the mountains where I was born and grew up.

My mother tells me that those rough mountain paths (as city-folk would call them today) ate away at her feet, and that the wind was so strong that one day it carried her from one side of the valley to the other. When she was six or seven years old, her mother emigrated to America (it was the practice in those days for our women to emigrate to work without their husbands from sheer poverty), and she suddenly became responsible for household affairs, as well as having to take provisions down to the bottom of the valley or up to the hills, where her father and eldest brother were working.

By way of comparison with our easy life today, she tells how her father sent this brother of hers out behind a herd of goats one day before daybreak. It was around October, when mist gathers on our mountains. Her brother came back before sunrise, after her father had gone to the fields. He told her that a wolf had attacked the herd, eaten some of the goats and scattered the rest. He was confused and afraid, because he could not round up the herd in the thick mist. She told him not to tell anyone and went back with him up to the high slopes, where they spent the day chasing the scattered goats until they had rounded them all up, except for two of them.

'Don't worry!' she said to him, 'I'll tell your father.'

My mother got married after her own mother had returned from America with the fruits of ten years' work.

Mr Kawabata,

I told you before, and I confirm to you now: I can define for you the precise colour of each day that I have lived. What is more, I can also define the precise colour of each night that has passed over my eyes for the past fifty years (which is how old I am) until today.

I quite understand that nobody else besides you will believe this. Apart from you, I don't know anyone who will accept that I can delve back into my memory moment by moment, as if I were in front of a book, turning over its pages at will.

Mr Kawabata,

You now know why I am addressing my words to you alone, among all my fellow-Arabs. I sometimes wonder what would have happened if you had not existed, and I am afraid. Is it, I wonder, that you have set me free, through the act you undertook in the last moment of your life?

Then again, as you probably know, my fellow-Arabs' lack of belief in me is not because they are convinced of the merits of forgetting, or of its necessity for the sake of progress. They are generally fed on memory, on Memory in fact – the Memory that we Arabs were once masters of the earth. It is for this reason that 'Revival' is the objective around which political discourse (and also literature) generally revolves.

My fellow-Arabs know the future well, because the image of it is already in their minds. It is the past as they like to see it, and as they would like it to be.

If these people have a problem, the reasons for it are already known. If they suffer, it is from a bitterness within themselves, brought about by their inability to fulfil their clear, well-defined desires. But the pain I am talking to you about is not like that.

If someone said that my condition was a rare one, I would probably agree. But you at least would surely not say that the rarity of a condition was a reason for regarding it as an illness – *we Arabs don't yet have hospitals for mental 'illnesses'*.

Why should the fact that something is rare arouse suspicion?

Why do my fellow-Arabs not believe me when I talk about my ability to remember?

Why are they so inclined to accept things that are similar, but not something that is unique?

When I put my argument to them, they call it fiction or make-believe. *When that happens I understand the bitterness of the Prophets!*

How, then, can I persuade them of an indisputable fact, namely that I can remember the time of my birth moment by moment. In fact, I can actually remember when my parents were married, and the moment they came together for my conception. *I will tell you in detail without delay how it happened, and you will be amazed that any reasonable man could refuse to believe what I say.*

How can I persuade them that my power of recollection is a natural gift that I am trying to turn to good use, to define where my pain lies?

How can I convince them of my pain? How convince them that most pains pale into insignificance beside it?

Mr Kawabata, you understand why I am writing to you. Listen:

My father inherited the house where he was born, where his brothers and sisters were born, and where we, his children, were also born.

It was in this house that he spent his honeymoon with his new wife (my mother), and the wedding celebrations that my aunt arranged with the help of some neighbours were also held there.

On the first night of their wedding, everyone went away after the festivities had ended, except for my aunt, who busied herself clearing away the table and washing up, helped by the bride, my mother.

My father stayed sitting on a chair, watching pensively.

My aunt was telling my mother where things should go.

Midnight passed and my aunt had still not left. She sat on a chair resting a little while my mother, the bride, stayed standing like a stranger, shy and confused. The three of them stayed like that, silent and pensive for a long time, despite the fact that everything had been agreed in advance between my father (the bridegroom), my aunt and the neighbours. It had been agreed that my aunt would sleep the first four or five nights at the neighbours' house. What had happened, then? How long would this situation continue?

The three of them remained pensive and silent for a considerable time.

The house consisted of a single large room, with an outside toilet, and the cooking was done in front of the door when the weather was fine. Were the three of them to sleep like that, then, with one of them standing from embarrassment and the other two sitting on chairs?

My mother was thinking of nothing at all. She was simply feeling a little tired after a very long day, but it was a tiredness she could bear. She was not waiting or expecting my father to say anything at all to her – not even, 'Sit down,' for example. Nor did it occur to my father to say to her, 'Sit down.' It was for my aunt to make the first move, but she did not.

Fortunately for everyone, in came the neighbour at whose house it had been agreed my aunt would sleep. She pointed out to my aunt that the night was far advanced, that she (the neighbour, that is) could not stay up any longer, and that the bride and groom must be exhausted.

At first my aunt refused, saying that she could manage here – that is, in the family home her brother had inherited. But she finally gave in and went off to sleep outside the house for the first time in her life. She was one year older than my father.

After my aunt had gone away, my father stayed sitting

silently, and my mother stayed standing silently.

My father had not even washed his mouth out, and nor had my mother.

My father had washed all over the night before, and so had my mother.

Then my father moved, and got up from his chair – not to approach his bride, but to spread out the bedding on the floor and sit on it.

My mother did not dare go near the bedding to lie down and recover from the exhaustion of the long day, but sat on a chair at a distance.

So they remained.

Then they heard the sound of footsteps outside, and perhaps a whisper as well, which made them stay even more firmly in their respective places. The door and two windows of the house were all full of holes that allowed anyone outside, who wanted to, to see everything inside. The only lamp in the house, which hung from the ceiling, was lit.

Then the sound of the footsteps receded, apparently into the distance.

After the footsteps had gone, my mother wanted to tell my father to lie down and sleep because she wouldn't be able to sleep. But she couldn't utter a single word. She was sitting with her arms folded, unable to look at my father properly, even out of the corner of her eye. She could only guess he was sitting there. My father couldn't find anything to say either, not a single word. Eventually the light of dawn caught up with them as they dozed: she was on a chair with her back leaning against the wall, while he was resting on his shoulder on the bed, but still in a sitting position.

My mother opened her eyes first and got up from the chair. Then my father opened his eyes as well and immediately glanced at the light, which was still lit. He pointed at the switch and my mother went and turned it off.

I remember well.

Nothing happened to my mother like the things that happened to other married couples – things that I began to hear about from boys older than myself as I started to grow up.

I never remember my father going out like other newlyweds in his cotton vest to buy two bananas from the shop, one for him and one for my mother, or some other food known for its invigorating effect.

*When I say 'I don't remember', Mr Kawabata, that means that it did not happen.*

But I do remember my father beating me at the age of six, when I was not expecting him to.

I pulled at the door to open it, but it would not open. I pulled it harder but it still wouldn't open. I pulled it so hard that I nearly pulled it off its hinges, before it occurred to me that it might be locked from the inside. How was I supposed to realize it was locked immediately? That was something that happened only very rarely. The door of our house was only locked with a key once in a blue moon. Suddenly the door opened while I was still pulling at it and my father appeared, drawing himself up to his full height. In his left hand he held a piece of bread with sugar on it, while with his right hand he beat me once, then a second time, on the head and cheek.

At the time I did not feel it. Later I called it injustice. Later still I sometimes called it victimization.

I did not go into the house after my father had come out. I only went back some hours later, in the evening. I remember well that I did not eat that night.

Sir,

My older friends claimed that *that* happened at night, when everyone was asleep. The man would come quietly, careful not to make a noise, and would slip into the woman's bed. But...

But how could I believe what they said, Mr Kawabata, when our house, like most of their houses, consisted of a single room? My mother would lay some mats out in the middle of the room, then spread mattresses on them for us to sleep on – herself in the middle, myself on her left, and my sister and brother (who was still being breast-fed) on her right. Her belly was swollen with another child – God willing, it would be a boy. Meanwhile, my father slept on a mattress beside the wall at our feet.

As for my aunt, my father built a room for her on the roof with his own hands after his marriage.

My schoolfriends had another story on the same subject. The man would give a sign to the woman while everyone was asleep, and the woman would get up quietly, careful not to attract any attention, and slip into the man's bed; then they touched each other and were both filled with a strange power. They made loud, strange noises that would wake anyone else who was sleeping, so they both put a piece of cloth in their mouth between their teeth and bit on it until they had finished.

They were so exhausted by this that they would sometimes accidentally fall asleep until morning and be surprised in the same bed.

Sir,

When I was young, I would often be restless at night. I would start to listen to whatever was going on, especially outside the house, and especially in summer when both windows were left open. I would watch the stars through the open windows for a long time, listening at the same time to the sounds of nocturnal animals – foxes, frogs and cockroaches, as well as other sorts of creatures whose names and shapes I did not know.

Even the birds sometimes made cheeping noises in the middle of the night like those they made during the day.

Sometimes during the night I would hear a woman's voice coming to me from under a thousand blankets, from behind a thousand doors.

I asked my schoolfriends whether they could hear what I heard, but they said no. Some of them tried to stay awake to find out whether what I said was true, but they fell asleep.

Then one of them who was older than us managed to persuade us all to stay up in a group and to keep awake until we heard the sound together. The summer was beautiful and the sky was clear. The meeting place was a house whose owners had left it some time ago. Its mud roof had collapsed, with some of its upper walls. At a certain moment during the night – none of us had a watch – I thought that I could hear a quiet noise that reminded me of the sound we were waiting for. But it was coming from somewhere very close. I could hear a whisper.

Two lips were moving slowly, with a panting rhythm. Our bodies were just beginning to develop. No hair and no sperm.

After that we continued waiting until we were overtaken by the light of dawn. We went back home before anyone woke, and crept back to our families pretending that we had been asleep since evening.

No!

That never happened to my mother. I remember...

We were playing a few feet from the house in the narrow street (I did not think of it as narrow at the time) between the houses of the quarter that were almost piled on top of one another. We stopped playing when we heard the frantic knocking on the door. It was my aunt thumping with her fist on the door – which, unusually, had been bolted. Her face and neck had turned red. When no one opened the door for her, she tried to open it by force.

Her persistence puzzled me.

Her frantic knocking on the door continued for some minutes. Instead of stopping, she went on knocking even harder and more insistently, calling her brother by name in a voice that was more like a shout, asking him why he would not open.

Some minutes went by. We thought that she had given up. But far from giving up, she had started trying to wrench off the door, pulling at one of its two halves until she had separated it slightly from the other one. When she was no longer able to continue, she left it to bang around and went away.

A few minutes after she had left, my father came out in his white cotton shirt. He looked to the right and to the left, calling his sister by name, asking her (even before he could see her) what she wanted. Suddenly she appeared from behind a house, asking him angrily, as she made for the door, why he would not open up, and telling him off for sleeping the whole day. My father did not reply, and my aunt went in.

My schoolfriends and I had stopped playing and, without wanting to, had been drawn into what was going on. Although I was not actually looking at them,

I could sense every single one of my friends staring in amazement.

For a long time after that incident, Mr Kawabata, I continued to wonder, rather regretfully, why my father had not said anything in reply – replied, for example, that he was taking his midday siesta, as he did every day after lunch when he was not working.

And my mother? What was my mother doing all this time? Had she buried her head under the bedclothes so as not to see or be seen? Or had she been embarrassed to stay in bed, got up and walked round to the lavatory by the back door, to make people think that she was washing or going to the toilet?

Then my aunt left the house quietly, like someone who has woken up from a long siesta on a summer's afternoon.

Sir,

A year after my parents' wedding, my mother gave birth to a girl, my elder sister. A year after that, I was born.

When one of the women came out to tell my father that the child was a girl, he was sure of that already, for the delivery had been relatively easy. He had heard the cries when he was in the street near the house walking up and down, obviously nervous. More important than that was his intuition. He had guessed for some time that it would be a girl. Wasn't it he who had said to the midwife when he went to ask her to come to the house: 'You needn't hurry; it's a girl!' In reply, the midwife had ticked him off for being like three-quarters of men, who only see the black side of things.

When my mother became pregnant for the second time, he was so happy he could not believe it. He waited impatiently for his wish to be fulfilled: a male child — myself!

He was certain that my mother would have a boy — so certain that he went and recorded me in the register of births three months before I was born. I was actually born at the end of March, though on my identity card it is stated that I was born at the beginning of January. My father wasn't working at the time, because it was wet and cold. So he took the opportunity to register me with his friend who worked in the relevant department. 'Why not?' his friend said. 'Let's create an accomplished fact. Rashid. After the name of his uncle who died childless in America.' 'OK,' said my father.

Mr Kawabata,

What I am telling you, you must accept without an iota of doubt. It is the truth.

Listen:

My birth took place a little before noon on a day towards the end of March. I can't tell you the precise time and date, because the practice then was not the same as it is today. Registering a birth by the minute, hour, day, month and year — that was all thought pointless.

I remember that something was pushing me in the direction of the open air. After a short while, my head collided with an obstruction, soft but firm. Then something began to tighten around my forehead, around the whole circumference of my skull. At that moment I began to feel cold on the top of my head. Then this thing tightened over my eyes, over my nose, my mouth, then over the rest of my body. But the head stage was the most difficult.

My feeling of cold increased as I slipped out. I saw...

As I slipped into this world, I saw everything that

caught my eye. I saw everything brightly and clearly, even though at that moment nothing had a name.

I saw, in the dim light, two naked thighs, open, taut and tensed. The legs were bent at the knees. I heard...

I heard the woman who caught me say: 'A boy!' in a tone whose meaning I understood later. My mother was very afraid that she would have a second girl. Then the midwife added: 'Rashid! You have your Rashid!' I started to hear my name repeated, and I was astonished to be called by a name.

As soon as I had emerged from my mother's womb – my mother was crying loudly – I found myself in a basin of lukewarm, slightly salty, water. I felt comfortable in this new environment and stretched myself out.

I remember well that I was very pleased to have emerged and I believe that the light made me happy. I recalled that, when I was still in my mother's womb, I used to like it when a little light reached me, I do not know how.

I saw some scissors.

Naturally, I cried a lot, but I was not crying because I was unhappy, so it didn't bother the women who were standing around us – around myself and my mother, that is.

I remember that the midwife had very clean hands and skin that was smooth to the touch. She was squatting in such a way that I could see all the parts of her body she hid from everyone except her husband (perhaps even from her husband). I was turned over several times in the bitter, salty, sticky fluid, which was beginning to smell; the least I can say about it today is that the smells were extremely unpleasant.

Then they wrapped me in clean, white swaddling bands, the same ones as had been used when my sister was born, the same ones my mother had lent during her pregnancy to her neighbour when she had a child. Then they handed me to my exhausted mother, who examined me carefully, running her hand over me to feel my skin.

Mr Kawabata,

My mother was born, grew up, got married and had several children, without knowing anything about this planet – that is to say, the earth.

My mother had never heard that the earth was round, or that it revolved, either on its own axis or around the sun. Until she sent me to school, she had never heard that every time the earth revolved it produced casualties and that it had been doing this from the very first revolution.

Until she sent me to school, I shared her belief.

I believed that everything in the universe was fixed for ever, just as it was, and that nothing would disturb the earth's harmonious relations with the other planets and stars until the end of time.

And that the end of time had no limit.

I used to believe that the few kilometres separating the mountains of Lebanon from the Mediterranean (mountains which, as we soon learned at school, had resulted from the piling up of earth brought down by torrential rains over a period of several thousand years) would never grow longer or shorter, higher or lower. Despite this, every winter, when the water ran cloudy from the tap in our house, I was worried. The rains were still carrying down the mud from the mountain tops then, the springs were becoming dirty and the river was turning red from its source to the sea. But...

But why *should* I change my belief, when there was nothing in creation that had not been ordered carefully, when everything suggested that we had finally entered the stage of eternal stability, and when nothing happened except by His command and His reckoning?

One evening, when my father raised to his eyes a glass filled from the tap in the house and looked at it carefully, like a priest contemplating the sacred chalice during communion, I was afraid!

Very afraid!

I asked myself a lot of questions. I wanted my father to talk to me and I wished I could talk to him. But instead he called my mother and showed her the water. My mother hurried to the tap. She filled a saucepan from it, which she put on the draining board so that the sediment could settle and we could use clean water for whatever we needed.

That night I dreamed of a long train that ran from the coast to the tops of the mountains, carrying sand and sprinkling it over the peaks. The sky was clear and the light was intense. I was in a ditch, which was neither deep nor wide and over which fell a black shadow. I was wearing only my underwear, my pants which my mother had sewn for me from one of the sacks of flour that the USA had sent to the Lebanon as food aid after the events of 1958. In this ditch, I looked just like the infant Jesus, as he was depicted in one of the pictures hanging in church. Like him, I was stretched out a little, but I was also raising my head slightly, like the new moon. I was waiting for my grandfather, but my grandfather did not come. People passed by without noticing me. This was impossible. I knew that I could not get out of the ditch by myself. So I stayed stretched out, silent but anxious, as people continued to pass me by.

The following morning the weather was fine. The sky was so clear that it delighted the heart. I got up, full of hope and certainty. The discoloration of the water from the previous evening had disappeared. This had been just dust, then, that the wind carried to the mountain-tops from distant places, or which fell from the trees in summer and autumn.

And dry grass, too.

And droppings from animals, birds and other living creatures.

But the peaks of the mountains remained as they were.

I got up in the morning and I could speak, so I asked my father whether the mountain peaks had remained as they had been since the time of his birth until the present day. He replied that they had not changed since God created them.

My mother also said that she could not remember them any different from the way they were now.

The day that the water at home turned cloudy in the tap, I did not know that the earth was round and that it revolved.

That it revolved, both on its own axis, and around the sun! I found that out later, in the lessons that followed.

*My father was sure of himself when he sent me to school, despite the succession of disturbing stories about what children learned there.*

As soon as the geography teacher told me about the earth, my heart beat faster and the colour drained from my face. I nearly fainted. The teacher realized, and stopped talking to ask what was the matter with me. When he saw that I was unable to speak, he hurried across to give me first aid, and sent a pupil to tell the caretaker and bring me a glass of water.

By the time the caretaker arrived, I was unable to breathe. I had lapsed into unconsciousness. He slapped me, then took hold of the muscles of my shoulders with both hands, and started to massage them. It hurt me, but my breathing improved, and I regained consciousness little by little. But when the glass of water arrived, it was cloudy!

It was winter at the time and it had been raining for days without stopping. Snow had already covered the mountain peaks and upper slopes and had begun to fall on the lower slopes as well. It had almost reached the coast, as the cold spell continued and grew more severe.

You must have breakfast every morning, the professor told me. You must have a hot drink and eat as they do in the developed world, in the West – meaning France (*only ten years had gone by since Lebanese independence and the French withdrawal*), where they get up in the morning in good time before they are due to go to work, then take a breakfast of coffee with milk, and slices of bread with a little butter and jam. Milk is a complete meal in itself, coffee is a stimulant and bread has the necessary calories.

That is how they have breakfast!

I hid my sorrow and embarrassment. In the morning I liked to eat the leftovers from my mother's cooking the previous day. I liked to eat a loaf of bread with a little *za'tar** on it, with some olives and olive oil. That is how I usually greeted the day. But progress has its price, and the task is a difficult one – the task of adapting to an advanced society. With self-discipline, however, we can overcome all difficulties.

I have never revealed to anyone that my fainting wasn't a medical problem, and no one noticed that the real reason for it was an emotional reaction that shook my whole being.

God!

How could it be that the earth was really a ball floating in space, just like that, with nothing supporting it and attached to nothing!

---

* crushed thyme and sesame seed

How could it be that the earth moved so quickly in its orbit around the sun? A hundred thousand kilometres in a single hour, no, eight thousand kilometres more than that, a hundred and eight thousand kilometres in a single hour!

The earth raced like a madwoman, but with indescribable precision, and so quickly that the brain could only imagine its speed. Yet despite this incredible speed, it took a whole year for it to complete a single revolution.

At the same time the earth revolved on its own axis ... so that the seasons repeated themselves.

Yes, now I understood:

It was not the centre of the universe, then, or the pivot of the heavens. Nothing supported it and no one carried it, neither man nor jinn nor the power of the Mighty One. The heavens above it had not been built, and the stars were not lamps suspended in the glassy canopy of the heavens. The heavens had no canopy. There was no heaven!

There was no heaven above the earth! The earth was a ball floating in space. It was simply one of the heavenly bodies too numerous to count.

My father was very sure of himself when he sent me to school, despite the succession of disturbing stories about it. But his attitude was clear (to him, at least), and his decision was final: I would leave school when I was able to read and write.

My mother was not bothered about the stories I brought back with me from school. As far as she was concerned, I was just a young boy who needed to repeat what was in the books that arrived from faraway places – books with things in them that boys needed to repeat until they got their certificate. The certificate itself was simply a passport to a steady job that would enable him to keep his fingernails clean.

A steady job was a thousand times better than the earth.

If the earth gave, it was after a thousand labours, and if it did not give, the worry lasted for days and days. But a steady job gave, pure and simple. If my mother had been given a choice before marrying, she would have chosen a husband with a steady job who received a salary at the end of each month – not a peasant or a barber (a village barber!) or a carpenter, or all three together as was the case with my father. She was bold enough once to tell me his name – the name of the man with a salary she would have chosen if... meanwhile she advised me, as usual, to study hard. I was embarrassed.

I was very embarrassed. My embarrassment lasted months, perhaps years (perhaps until today). Then as time went on this embarrassment turned into a deep sorrow.

The day she made her revelation, I asked her: 'Do you love his son more than me?'

I didn't pay any attention to her answer, because what she had told me had shaken me badly.

'Why do you kiss him whenever he comes to see me?'

I didn't tell her that his mother didn't kiss me when I went to his house. It wasn't embarrassment that stopped me, it was a deep desire for my mother to hate him with all her heart, to hate him as naturally as if it were breathing, to hate everything that might have happened and stopped her from having me as her son. And to act on the basis of this hatred.

I should never have been satisfied with my mother

stopping kissing his son just to spite *his* mother, or to repay her in kind. If only things were that simple!

My father, who was sure of himself, let these stories from school pass over his ears fleetingly at first.

Then he began to pretend he had not heard them.

In fact, however, he did hear them, I was quite sure that he heard them and paid attention to them.

My father was always long-suffering, but reluctantly so. He was very patient – by which I mean, he waited a long time to explode. But he certainly exploded in the end. Even when he died, he was very patient before dying, then he simply exploded and died. *When I stood beside his corpse, laid out in the middle of the house, surrounded by women all in black, I stood there without shedding a single tear. Meanwhile the others – my brothers and other relatives – were weeping and wailing over him. I stayed standing there watching the ancient rituals that no longer had any meaning. On future occasions, I again refused to accompany the procession to weep over the corpse. I did the same on the last occasion just before the corpse was carried away, because I couldn't play the part of the mourner while I was convinced that he had exploded and died.*

My father was long-suffering and taciturn, but reluctantly so. It would have been stronger on his part not to be so long-suffering before he exploded. But he couldn't behave in any other way.

Some years after I discovered that the earth was round, and that it revolved both on its own axis and around the sun, my father exchanged his Arab trousers for Western ones. A full year had elapsed by that time since Gagarin had circled the earth. Exchanging Arab trousers for Western ones attracted attention, and gave rise to sarcastic laughter that sometimes led to fist-fights and brawls. But my father did not involve us in any trouble. He acted wisely, and came through the experience with complete success which really did him credit. He persuaded the tailor who sewed his trousers for him to keep it secret. When the trousers were ready, he waited until midday on the Monday, when most people would be busy, before coming out; then, after wandering round the village streets in them, he took them off in the afternoon. For several days he repeated the same performance until finally he walked round in them during the afternoon, when people were sitting in front of their doors, waiting for the sun to set. He walked through every single lane in the village. After that he didn't wear Arab trousers again except when he was going to the fields.

I often tried to persuade him to go to work in the fields in Western trousers. I explained to him logically and rationally that he would find it easier, but he wasn't persuaded. He even scolded me, when he saw that my mad ideas wouldn't stop by themselves. He died without changing his ways.

Many people were angered by the stories that we (myself and my classmates, that is) brought back from school, but our neighbour Sadiq was by far the most argumentative. He used to lie in wait for us, and we could always reckon on meeting him at the same time – once a week, the day of the geography class. In addition, of course, to the chance meetings that happened often, very often.

Sadiq would take responsibility for speaking on their behalf.

Them.

Grown-ups, the older generation, people on whom

time had eaten and drunk. *This is an expression, Mr Kawabata, which our teacher used a lot.*

Fortunately, the geography class was the last period of the day – the day when we had a regular appointment, that is. As soon as the bell went, we were off.

Sadiq would stand on one foot and lift up the other one, pretending to be standing on a steep slope. One foot up and one foot down. Then he would stretch his hands out like wings and say: 'So this is how we stand on the earth, is it! Isn't this how we should stand, if the earth were like a ball, as you say it is?

'Why don't we fall off the earth's surface, then, if the earth is a ball floating in space?

'I'm fifty years old, and I've never seen the window of my house on the east side facing west. How *can* the earth revolve, then?

'God curse your schools and your teachers!

'And gravity?

'Gravity! God give you gravity!'

On many occasions voices were raised, and people would gather round us. Then the shopkeeper in front of whose door we were gathered would drive us away, and ask Sadiq and his allies – the 'older generation' – to calm down. When we refused to listen, and insisted on continuing the argument, his wife would throw water at us. We would go away laughing noisily, pretending that we were about to fall off the surface of the earth, imitating Sadiq's movements as he demonstrated to us how a man would stand if the earth really was a ball.

'We go round so fast we become dizzy, then,' Sadiq would repeat, putting his hand on his brow and closing his eyes as he pretended to be trying not to fall over from vertigo.

The most insistent and impetuous one of us was

Jamil. Sometimes his impetuosity led him to grab Sadiq by the trousers, in an attempt to make him lose his balance and bring him to the ground. Our friends laughed, but when Jamil's mother heard about it she rushed out angrily, with face and neck flushed red, and threw one of her shoes at him. Then she would shout at him, cursing God and blaming Him for taking her husband, Jamil's father, who had been killed during one of the periodic flare-ups of a feud between the different families in the area. His father had been a strong-arm for one of the families. Men from a rival family had ambushed him and opened fire on him, and he had fallen dead before he was able to use his weapon – the revolver which he always kept by his side. *My father would constantly insist that after his death we should put his revolver under the pillow he rested his head on, because that was the only thing he had faith in, even in his final agony.*

'Otherwise, it will be like burying me naked.'

Because Jamil's father unfortunately hadn't been able to use his weapon, his revolver wasn't put under the pillow he laid his head on for the last time after his death. That was as he had wished it.

Jamil's father was quite determined that his soul should be punished for his shortcomings.

Jamil would run away from his mother but she would catch him up. He would follow her, then she would go back to her house and he would come back to us, doubly victorious, to continue the argument.

This Jamil was also killed. He was with us in school when armed men entered the classroom, called his name and made him go out. He was ashen-faced as he left but I shall never forget how he remained silent and composed.

The teacher went out behind them but came back

quickly, in an agitated state.

Then, after about half an hour, during which time the teacher had continued to try to stay calm, we heard a single shot. Jamil had been shot in the head from behind.

Jamil had been made to stand with his face to the wall of the church. When news came that a wounded gunman had died, the dead man's brother came forward and fired a single shot into him from his revolver.

I couldn't attend the funeral because it took place in their part of the town. I couldn't express a desire to go, or even hint at it.

I can tell you, Mr Kawabata, that most people in our part of town were satisfied with the speed of the response to the loss of one of our people. Some people were so satisfied you might say they were happy. Because the enemy had lost someone whose death would lead to more tears in mothers' eyes than our dead man. Our dead man was an illiterate man of nearly sixty, whereas theirs was a young schoolboy of just sixteen years.

'God forbid, a child!' the more partisan of our family would repeat, pretending that they were mourning him like his mother and relatives.

How I wanted to see him before he was buried. I went to visit his mother secretly on a mad impulse a few days after his death. The blood rushed to her face and she screamed when she saw me. I left immediately, before the neighbours arrived to see what she was shouting about, and I waited anxiously for several days after that for the news to spread, but she had said nothing.

Sadiq complained to my father about me more than once, I knew that, though of course my father didn't say anything to me. My father was never ever present at our squabbles, because he could never stomach what went on in them.

My father knew every detail of what was going on, but he stayed silent. It was a pretended ignorance, disturbingly natural. He would turn a blind eye to things for the moment, but would never let go of them entirely. And it was all precisely calculated!

I felt deeply disturbed – more so every day – by his long silence, which had lasted much longer than was usually the case with him. I felt that the explosion had simply been delayed.

And this uncertainty disturbed me.

Until one day he came to me and asked me to read him a letter which he had received from my uncle's wife in America. I took it from him and started to look at it for a while, leaning my head now to the right and now to the left, opening my eyes wide, then narrowing them, as if I were trying to peer into the far distance. I began to read but stumbled several times, hesitating on several words and letters. He shook his head and said that I had to learn not only to read a letter, but also to write one.

My father read only with difficulty, and he never wrote. He knew only how to sign his name, and he used to boast about this to my mother. He always used to say that, if circumstances had permitted, and he had learned to read and write, he would have been good at it, and would have been much better off by now.

When he said this, my mother would take the opportunity to repeat a phrase from a song of Farid al-Atrash: *But 'if only' never built a house.*

This phrase gave rise to bitter arguments between the two of them which lasted for years. We – the children, that is – watched these arguments with terrible feelings of fear, trepidation and embarrassment.

During these quarrels my mother would boast to him that she had never wanted to marry him, that her family had forced her to, and that...and that...He would come out with whatever replies he felt like making. Finally, the situation would be resolved by my mother uttering her pet phrase without further comment when she thought that the situation called for it. My father would avoid replying or exacerbating the situation, so long as she stuck to the same phrase, but without humming it – if she hummed it, it provoked my father even more!

Several months had passed since the day when my father had come to ask me to read that famous letter from my uncle, but he had not repeated the request.

The first months were especially long. I was miserable because of the waiting, having to be on my guard and planning for a confrontation. Then gradually I began to forget, especially as by that time Sadiq's opposition to our stories and ideas had softened, not because he was persuaded but because he was tired.

We had worn him out.

So much so that when we sought him out after the geography class to tell him the new things we had learned about the universe, he would content himself with repeating in front of us: 'I am certain that I am going to die!'

Just that.

He would content himself with this phrase, after which he would keep a stubborn silence and we would go away, having failed to stir him to say anything else. Once he said to us: 'The pains you feel now when you are young will vanish quickly like a passing illness. But they are the beginning of the disease that will destroy you in the future, when you are older.'

Sometimes, he would describe us as immortal.

When we went on at him until he was unable to hide his anger, he would say (directing his words at me) that if I had been his son, he would have branded me – yes, branded me – with a red-hot rod of iron.

We scored a resounding victory when Gagarin's spaceship circled the earth that historic day in 1961. It was impossible to deny this fact, just as it was impossible to deny that the sun gave light to the earth, heating it in winter and scorching it in summer.

Sadiq didn't deny this fact, but he didn't acknowledge it either. He simply kept silent. His silence was both terrible and provocative.

This made me angry.

I remember.

Jamil would turn the radio up to its loudest when the news broadcasts started, so that Sadiq – whose house was about fifty yards away – could hear. *Jamil had taken charge of the radio at home after his father had been killed, and his mother didn't try to interfere.*

At that time we didn't know about transistor radios or television, of course.

Sadiq, who usually worked outside his front door, took his work inside the house, and stayed there for several days until the broadcasts stopped talking about Gagarin's voyage.

Sadiq made me angry! He made me very angry! Why wouldn't he be convinced, why wouldn't he admit the truth, why wouldn't he accept it?

I remember –

The day after that great day I bought a newspaper for the first time in my life. The first page was indeed about Gagarin's historic voyage into space around the earth. It was full of pictures and news, especially pictures. I read everything written in the newspaper about the event, on my way home from the place where newspapers were sold. I gobbled it up. My heart was beating quickly, powerfully, from deep inside me. I could hear the beats as if they were magical voices rising from a deep valley.

I looked at the pictures.

Pictures of my brother Gagarin. My schoolmate and classmate Gagarin!

Dear Mr Kawabata, how can I describe to you the relationship between Gagarin and myself at that moment? He was part of me, I was him and he was me. For a long time we would go to school together, come back together, sleep together, eat together, and swim together in the river near our house. I could ask him for light during the darkest part of the night as I walked in the dark streets. I needed no light while his rays lit my being, and his light poured out before me on the road.

I am certain of that, Mr Kawabata, I am certain. I am also certain that you believe me without an atom of doubt, now that you know me and know my amazing powers of recollection. What I am telling you is actual fact.

I threaded the needle in the night with his light. I put the thread in the eye of the needle, as easily as putting my finger in my fist. I repeated it several times. All my friends witnessed it. If necessary, I can ask those of them who are still alive today to confirm it. *Life has gone quickly, Mr Kawabata! Many of them have died!*

Sadiq didn't read and he didn't write. He couldn't distinguish an *alif*★ from a telegraph pole. But I showed

---

★ ‏ا‎ First letter of the alphabet

him the pictures. I said to him, 'Look!' My heart was still thumping, and I was still panting as if I had just run all the way across the steppes of Asia. He looked at the pictures, but he gave no indication of having understood anything. I read him what had been written, then I showed him the pictures again. I put them under his eyes as he bent over the basket he was making with strips of cane. He thrust them away from in front of his face with his fist, while still looking at them out of the corner of his eye. Then I cut the pictures from the newspaper. I went into his house and put them on his pillow.

Unfortunately for me, there wasn't a single picture among them showing the whole earth as a ball floating in space, with nothing supporting it and without anything above it pulling it up – a decisive picture taken by Gagarin with his own hand from space, that would settle the matter once and for all. This was what I had been dreaming of as I went to buy the newspaper. I was wanting to see the picture with my own eyes, so that my heart could be at peace for ever, because Sadiq could always come up with an objection to the truth, however obvious it was.

He followed me as I went into his house. I saw him as I was turning around to go back, after I'd put the pictures on his pillow so that he wouldn't be able to ignore them when he wanted to rest his head.

I saw him!

Standing in the middle of his house, with a thick cane in his hand. When I reached him, he came down on me with a blow to my side. I doubled up, and he hit me a second blow on the back. Then the blows came even thicker and faster, with all the nervous energy he could muster, until the cane snapped on my body. 'You want me to change my beliefs when I've already come to the end of my life!' he said, before throwing the cane from his hand. 'I've no son to comfort me, and I've left not a single thing behind for people to remember me by. I have one hope left, the hope of heaven, and you want me to lose that?'

I didn't say a single word, either while he was speaking to me or while he was beating me. I didn't shout with pain, anguish or any other emotion. I just put a brave face on it, held my peace and went out.

This incident ruined the geography lesson for me. It always came back to me in every detail as soon as the lesson started. Sadiq's words would start to buzz around my ears, distracting me from following what the teacher was saying. The teacher noticed that I had changed and asked me what was wrong. I didn't give him a clear-cut answer, but later I asked him what it was that made old people refuse to accept these facts. His reply was that they had had their day – *Mr Kawabata, this expression, 'they had had their day', is the sort of expression that I have been eager to call to your attention, although it is most often to be heard on the lips of leftists, 'progressives' and intellectuals generally* – and he added some harsh but polite words about them. He said that if our fathers and grandfathers had been different, we wouldn't have ended up in this state of backwardness, where we'd been left behind by the rest of the world in everything: the invention of the car, the aeroplane, electricity, the telephone, the atom . . . *The geography teacher was very fond of this word 'invention'.* If our brains hadn't been so stupid, we could have overtaken every other country, or at least been equal with them. But our ancestors were tied to the earth's surface, shackled by its gravity, untroubled by any questions, with hearts that took no pleasure in reality. Take the pearls in the sea – the man that risks all to dive for them, can reach them and bring them back to land; but the man that stays on the surface of the water by the shore, comes back with only a hidden longing. Our ancestors stayed on the shore. Before the development of science, people used to die for the most trivial reason. Appendicitis used to finish off thousands. A single pill taken once a day can save you from death or illness.

'Where is God, then?' one of his pupils asked him one day.

This was a question, if truth be told, that I too had hidden in my heart. I say 'hidden', because I was afraid to expose it, in case an open struggle should break out in my emotions, between scientific truth and God: I loved scientific truth in a way that made my heart race, and I feared for God in a way that made my bones tremble. I was sure that this was the case with every pupil.

'God is everywhere! God is Spirit!' answered the teacher.

The answer was refreshing, but it was not enough. I was not completely satisfied. I still felt a hidden thirst which lasted for a long time – several years, in fact – I mean, until I read (*we* read, to be more precise) the play *The Life of Galileo* by Brecht, by the communist playwright, comrade Bertold Brecht. On that day...

On that day, I well remember (I, who never forget) – I remember how we learned the play off by heart. His friend Sagredo says to Galileo: 'I tremble with fear that this may be the truth!' – *i.e. that the earth may be simply another planet and not the centre of the universe.*

'Where is God, then?' Sagredo continues. 'Where is His throne? Where does it rest?'

Galileo: 'What do you mean?'

Galileo knew that to deny the existence of God meant death.

Sagredo: 'God! Where is God?'

Galileo: 'He is not up there, anyway.'

'Where is He, then?' his friend asks.

Galileo: 'Within ourselves, or nowhere!'

'That is what the unbelievers say,' says Sagredo. 'They deserve to have their blood spilled.'

We liked the way Galileo spoke about reason and mankind, Mr Kawabata. We particularly liked it when he said that only the dead were unmoved by scientific proofs, for how could a living being resist their allure?

The supremacy of reason is the salvation of the masses!

Galileo: I need Andrea [the servant's son].

Mrs Sarti (the servant): Andrea? He's in bed, almost asleep.

Galileo: Wake him up!

Wake him up!

People will come to know the truth about the heavens, and they will realize how many other facts they are ignorant of. And so one day they will decide to open their eyes wide!

My reading of Brecht's play was one of the most beautiful gifts life has given me. During that period life gave generously: Gagarin's orbit of the earth in outer space, the victory of the Cuban revolution, the legendary brilliance of the Algerian revolution, and before that the nationalization of the Suez canal. But Brecht's gift had a very special impact, and a very special aroma, for it helped me to conquer my deep-seated, persistent feeling of guilt and sorrow that had grown in me following the memorable incident with Sadiq. His answer hurt me deeply, despite the fact that it never made me change my mind, or left any impression on me. Nevertheless...

I was wounded by his hurt.

Perhaps wounds are transferred by contagion.

I had no arguments I could use to persuade him. I didn't know how to say to him that the misery mankind is groaning under now is not something for which a price can be paid later. So we have to put an end to its causes now, here on this earth, so that we can escape from it and be able to live happily. I had not yet read *The Life of Galileo*.

I wish I had read the play before the incident!

As well as the wound which the incident opened in my heart, it was a big mistake from a tactical point of view. It was a mistake that destroyed me through bitter experience.

I fell into the mistake knowingly, aware of its painful consequences, but avoiding it was something beyond my power and will. I was led on by an irresistible desire to strike while the iron was hot. In the decisive battle, one has to mobilize all the forces at one's disposal: I bought a newspaper!

And read it out loud!

To him!

I didn't tell anyone what had happened between Sadiq and myself. I was certain that he wouldn't tell anyone either, until some days later my father came to me with a letter in his hand, which he handed to me, asking me to read it to him. There was an insistence in his request which stopped me complaining, or expressing surprise, or refusing. In fact, he didn't so much *ask* me as *tell* me, in a way which suggested that there was not an iota of doubt in his mind about my ability to read. At first I tried to contain his insistence by hesitating a little. Then I opened the letter – it was dated a month previously – and began to read in a very hesitant and stumbling fashion.

'Read!' he said.

My reading had improved, but it was still poor. So he hit me, angrily and furiously. I told him that I wasn't used to reading handwriting and pointed out that I was able to read the newspaper only because it was printed like a schoolbook. So he hit me again.

My mother was at home, watching what was going on. I expected her to intervene vigorously to save me, but she merely raised her voice a little and said to him: 'You want to force him to read?' then left the house angrily.

What a disaster! How could she go out, leaving me on my own to face his anger?

My father had turned a dark colour, the same colour as when he was laid out after he had died. As he continued hitting me, my refusal became more stubborn.

He didn't once mention the newspaper. He didn't mention anything else either, nothing at all. He just continued insisting that I should read. 'Read!'

Harder than all this was the fact that he hadn't left me a bridge to retreat over. I couldn't retreat without a pretext, no matter how feeble, even though I wanted to with all my heart. In fact, it was he who didn't want me to retreat. This was clear to me, I had realized it almost from the first moment.

But retreat to where? And how? If I read clearly and quickly, that carried the danger that he might force me to leave school again, even though my mother was capable of confronting him and standing in his way when this subject became an issue.

My father's argument was that before long he would not be able to satisfy his family's needs on his own. My mother's argument when he was there was that 'God will provide'. Her argument when he was not there was that he wanted his children to live as he had lived, in disgrace. That was her expression.

Once she said it to his face. It was the first time, and he beat her.

I was thirteen years old. Spring was ending and summer beginning, and the official certificate examination results had arrived. I had failed. My marks were reasonable in every subject, except for dictation and questions in French, where they were zero. My father made his decision at once: I had to leave school and learn a trade. He asked me which trade I wanted to learn but I refused to answer the question at all, because I was fundamentally opposed to the idea. What I wanted was simply to continue my studies, despite the fact that I had failed. In truth, this failure didn't represent a mistake or incompetence on my part. We simply had no French language teacher in the school, so we would spend the French period with the games teacher in the playground, or else be sent home.

One day, a French-language teacher was brought to us, who was very fond of Corneille's play *Le Cid* (Corneille, of course, being one of the greatest seventeenth-century French dramatists). For the whole school year he read us the text of the play in an Arabic translation and explained it to us, comparing it with the works of the Arab poet Abu al-Tayyib al-Mutanabbi.

The teacher was very fond of the character of Rodrigue (with Chimène, the main character in the play). He was always saying that if Rodrigue had been born an Arab, he would have been like al-Mutanabbi.

We dwelt for a whole month on the one sentence he knew by heart in French – '*La valeur n'attend pas le nombre des années*' – while he commented on it and compared it with some verses of al-Mutanabbi.

He would also often digress and switch from subject to subject, until we had forgotten where we started. We passed from Chimène's housekeeper – who explained to her sincerely and truthfully the characteristics of each of her two suitors, Rodrigue and his rival – to how women among us tell lies when they want to persuade a young man to marry a young woman (or the opposite) – so that a girl with loose morals, for example, may be depicted as a saint. Or the opposite. A friend of his once told him that he was in love with a quiet and beautiful girl and wanted to marry her. He managed to convey his friend's wishes to the girl, so she invited him to go to her family's house and ask them for her hand. He agreed. In the course of the visit, he was talking with her family about various things, but had not yet got round to the subject he had come for. The girl brought coffee in, wearing the prettiest dress she had, and offered him a cup. At this point he decided to put her to the test, so he purposely spilled the cup of coffee over her dress as he took it from her. (Naturally, he pretended that it was an accident.) The girl carried on smiling, and even tried to set his mind at rest when she saw him apologizing and showing that he felt guilty, then went back to the kitchen to bring him a towel, and a rag to wipe the floor with. Then she came back in again with another cup of coffee, which he took and placed on the small table in front of him. He then stood up and asked if he could go into the kitchen to drink a glass of water. She begged him to stay where he was so that she could bring it to him immediately, but he gave her the slip and sneaked into the kitchen, where he caught sight of a wooden table with teethmarks on it. She had been so furious that she had bitten the edge of the table when the coffee had spilled over her pretty dress, although in front of him she had pretended exactly the opposite. The man thanked God in his heart and went back in, not knowing how he would finish his coffee or bring the visit to an end. He went out without speaking about the business he had come for, and never returned.

The French teacher needed a quarter of an hour to start his lesson. First of all he would get a piece of yellow cloth out of his bag, the sort that drivers use to clean their cars. He would use it to wipe the dust off the chair, then off the desk, and would then put his bag on the desk and get the rest of his things out of it. Then, with the help of a ruler, he would very slowly draw on the board some lines, fine and almost invisible, so that he could write straight. He actually seldom wrote. Then he would stare at the pupils for a long time, until he caught sight of something he did not like, which he would go on about at great length. Once he noticed my toes sticking out of my shoes and socks. My shoes were so old that the soles were coming away from the leather. He asked me why I didn't get my shoes mended. I didn't give him an answer, so he repeated the question. I told him that they were very old and that my father had promised me a new pair soon. 'No, no, no!' he said. 'We shouldn't be ashamed of what is old. The Queen of England used to buy the newest and most expensive clothes for her children and deliberately rip them at the neck – *where clothes wear out first* – and mend them again. Then she let her children on to the street like that, to prove to everyone that it is not poverty that is a fault, but bad behaviour.'

Unfortunately, the French dictation exercise and the questions on it in the official examination at the end of the year bore no resemblance to what our teacher had been teaching us. Most of us failed. The only ones to pass were a few students whose families knew some French already.

None of these explanations or interpretations carried any weight in my father's view, however. His mind was made up. What was decreed in his eyes was decreed. He tried, gently, to persuade my mother, telling her that if Rashid began to learn a trade now, he would be able to help us later, so that his brothers would be able to pursue their studies. *There were five of us by that time: three girls and two boys.* My mother rejected his arguments, for she couldn't imagine dirt under the nails of any of her children (*that was how she referred to manual labour*). When she saw my father going on about it like that, she screamed at him: 'I won't let my children live as you've made us live, in disgrace!'

– 'In disgrace!'

She spat blood, her nose started to bleed, and her eye was swollen for a whole month. If it hadn't been for the grace of God, she would have gone blind.

It was then decided that my trade should be that of motor mechanic. I actually spent a year fixing cars. It was a miserable year at first, not because I didn't like the trade but because I wanted to continue studying. I was missing the geography lessons.

What had become of the earth, then, and the moon, and the sun, and gravity, and the vast expanse of the universe, and the stars which had disappeared though their light still reached us? And the truth, the liberating truth?

For the first few weeks of that year learning a trade, I received a paltry sum of money at the end of each week. As time went on, the sum increased, but it never reached any great value even at the end. I would always offer it to my mother, but she would say to me: 'Spend it as you like.' The thing I liked most was the cinema. I went a lot to the cinema, at least once every week, and the money was enough for that.

I don't want to make myself seem superior to other people, Mr Kawabata, but I have to tell you that I was secretly quite amazed when the cinema hall burst into laughter as we watched a Charlie Chaplin film. I couldn't fathom what it was about these films that made other people laugh, when they made me cry. I was also secretly embarrassed by my friends' disclosures that they were excited by the film stars in the films we were watching, and that they fantasized and dreamed about them when they were alone. To me they were pure saints, whose troubles were my troubles and whose pain was my pain.

Every evening my mother would wash my oil- and grease-stained clothes with her own hands. In complete silence. Her silence would be even more obvious when my father was there.

One day in the middle of spring my father said to me: 'Next year you'll go back to school.' It was evening, and my mother was preparing supper with a radiant expression on her face that I hadn't seen since I started work. I was so surprised that my heart missed a beat. I had mixed feelings. I would be returning to the sources of knowledge, but at the same time I'd be leaving a trade that I'd begun to like and become skilled at, and would also be leaving behind my evening freedom and the cinema.

I didn't ask that evening what had caused him to change his mind. When I asked my mother a few days later, her reply was unconvincing: 'Isn't school cleaner?'

Some years later I realized what had happened to change my father's mind. I had begun learning the trade in the middle of summer. In the middle of autumn, at the height of the olive-picking season, my father had been attacked. He had gone with some farmworkers into the olive grove we owned and noticed that a number of olive trees had been partly stripped. When evening fell, the guard came demanding his payment as usual, but my father refused to pay him because he hadn't done his duty. *My father was always accusing this guard of stealing.* Their disagreement turned into a fight, in the course of which the guard, who was a lot younger than my father, managed to get the better of him by hitting him hard several times with a thick stick. The injury was more psychological than physical, despite the fact that my father himself had been unarmed.

My father only told my mother about this some days later, after she had begun to notice a change in him – and a particular interest in his revolver. She asked him about it repeatedly. My mother's anger had upset her considerably, but she kept it under control so as not to encourage my father to carry out what he seemed to be planning. For several days she carried on trying to be nice to him. So they made up, and I left work in the middle of summer, after she had spent several months persuading him. I returned to school at the beginning of October and the geography classes restarted, souring my relationship with Sadiq once again.

In that same year, Gagarin made his momentous orbit of the earth in outer space. 'Read,' said my father. My stubbornness, however, was stronger than my desire to read – stronger than all the painful blows and the humiliation they represented.

Finally, my father resorted to a rope, which he used to tie me to the chair before putting the letter in front of my eyes. The letter was from America, from the wife of his brother (my uncle) and was full of hostility and abuse, accusation and counter-accusation. It said that my father spent his time begetting children rather than working, then asked his sister-in-law to pay for their education. If she had wanted to spend her money on children, it said, she could have had as many of her own as she wanted.

In fact, my uncle's wife was bragging, as she hadn't been able to have children at all— either through her fault or that of her husband who had died young at the age of thirty and after whom I was named.

After my father had tied me up, he lit the gas fire and put a skewer on it of the sort we use for cooking meat. His intention was obvious –

Either I read well, or he would brand my fingers with the skewer that was turning red on the fire.

He had made up his mind to brand my fingers after he'd become convinced that I could actually read well but was hiding the fact from him so that he wouldn't force me to leave school.

There had been warning signs from him to that effect for some time. When I came back from school at the end of the day, I would usually dump my books, go out to meet my friends, and stay outside until it became completely dark. If I came back to the house before the daylight outside had disappeared, I couldn't sleep. My father used to grumble at this habit of mine, on the grounds that when I studied in the evening, I used electricity. Normally, he would just grumble. But when the arguments flared up about whether the earth was round or rotated, he would grumble even more and insist that I turn off the light. Finally, he actually made me turn it off, and I was forced to study by the only light available to me – the light outside.

Those were sad moments of the day for me. My father knew that, and treated me harshly. He wanted me to leave school after I had learned to read and write properly. But he didn't express his wish openly, for fear of poisoning relations between himself and my mother again. He was pushing me to take the decision myself. He wanted to free me from the mistaken ideas I was learning in school. I realized that intuitively, and my intuition confirmed my mother's remarks and advice. Every time there was a crisis in my relationship with my father, she would advise me to go to church more often and to pray more. For my father, however, the question was no longer whether I should leave school to learn a trade; it had become deeper than that.

I knew that well, for I understood the secrets of his heart.

I don't believe that any child, boy or girl, could have fathomed the secrets of their father's heart as I did mine. My understanding of him was instinctive: I mean, he never ever surprised me with an action or reaction. I could almost see him going back to doing something before he had started to do it. I wasn't surprised, for example, when he handed me an empty glass and sent me to the station to fill it with petrol. I understood immediately that he was going to use it as medicine. I knew that he placed a high value on petrol, despite the fact that he despised other industrial substances, and that although he refused to use any other medicines he believed in the healing properties of petrol. In fact, he'd never really needed medicines until one day he complained of a headache which was diagnosed as being caused by worms in the stomach. This was a common complaint with us in those days – a complaint that the doctors attributed to eating raw meat, or to vegetables watered with sewage water.

When we were young, things that we called 'longworms' would sometimes slither slowly down our bare legs. They were white and sticky. We would make rude remarks to each other if any of us saw them on someone else's legs.

The only thing we knew about them was that they caused dizziness because they sucked the most nourishing substances from our stomachs. We had heard that there was an effective medicine for them and started to buy it and drink it without our family knowing, but my father preferred petrol.

My father preferred petrol for himself, but he didn't recommend it for us.

Mr Kawabata,

Who am I to tell the story of the worms to, if not you?

I am certain, indeed I am absolutely convinced, that if I told the story to anyone else, they would be sick! Christian or Muslim.

Especially women!

Especially if I told them how the worms used to collect in our trousers in their dozens. Then either the cotton would soak up the fluid, so that the worms became dry and stuck where they were, or else the worms would quickly crawl across and down our legs while they were still moist.

*Cleanliness, Mr Kawabata (you will allow me this remark about life in general), and pretending that bodily filth does not exist, undoubtedly represents a deep-seated desire among mankind to overcome his animal nature – I mean the animal*

*that is man himself. I regard fasting and the soul in the same*
*way. Does wisdom, then, mean pretending that this filth does*
*not exist, rising above it, and fixing one's gaze on a clean*
*'essence', while science fixes its gaze on filth ?*

*Mr Kawabata, listen to this also:*

*These stories often arouse a desire to vomit, and often turn*
*the stomach. If a Christian told them to a Muslim, the latter*
*would say 'you are all worm-eaten'. Conversely, if a Muslim*
*told them to a Christian, the latter would say the same.*
*Though of course, the Christians belong to different sects and*
*groups, and Muslims too!*

When my father's dizziness had persisted for some
time, he decided to treat it. So he drank a cup of petrol,
at one gulp. I was afraid he would die. His eyes were
closed and he staggered to a chair as his tongue touched
his bitter saliva. But instead of sitting down he went out
of the shop and began walking about, spitting. I was
behind him, following him a step at a time, trying to
avoid his seeing me. He put out his hand to me behind
him and pulled me towards him, smothering me. The
smell of petrol blocked my nostrils. I asked him what I
should do now, immediately. 'Nothing,' he replied.
Suddenly he doubled up and tried to empty his
stomach, but nothing came up. 'Do you want some
water?' I asked. 'No,' he said. I was extremely agitated,
but he just walked on. 'My heart is on fire,' was all he
said. 'Then we must do something,' I said. 'No,' he
replied. Eventually his eyes began to bulge, and his
eyelids would not close. We were some metres away
from the door of the house, trying desperately to reach
it. When we reached the door, he sat down on the steps
and gave a deep groan, trying unsuccessfully to close his
eyes. Then he gave a long sigh, got up and went inside.
He put the full weight of his body down on a chair,

which turned over as he fell with it. 'Don't be frightened!' he said, before getting up – before even trying to get up, 'I've only fallen over!' Then he got up and sat down on the chair. 'I'm going to tell mother,' I said – though in fact I had actually started running before I started speaking.

I will never forget how he smothered me, how he stretched out his hand behind him and pulled me towards him, and how he guessed exactly where I was standing in relation to himself. Whenever things grew tense between us, I remembered those moments. I particularly remembered them when he was being cruel to me and branding my fingers.

My father would brand my fingers with a red–hot iron, out of love for me – and, of course, out of love for the family, the country, his sect and his religion. If I had known Spinoza's famous aphorism then – the aphorism that says, 'You cannot compel anyone, by force or by law, to gain eternal happiness' – it would certainly have come to me then...

When my father loved, and showed his love, he captivated you, and his affection made the heart melt. He loved his children to be clean, but he was not too proud to soil himself in our filth. Once he ate a piece of bread without washing his hands, which had been soiled by my younger brother who had diarrhoea. He would kiss us on our noses which were streaming with a cold. He didn't ask our mother about her weaknesses towards us – a piece of chewing gum or a sweet, or something else that we were desperate for when we were young. Our mother would run after us. A gust of wind would shake the leaves on the tree, the tree would bear fruit, and the fruit, if it wasn't plucked when ripe, would fall to the ground and rot. Nature was nature. When our mother was pregnant, and people said to her.' You have too many children,' she would reply: 'What can I do with them? I can't leave them in my stomach!'

What can the tree do with its fruit, Mr Kawabata, and what can the fruit do with its ripeness? There is no doubt that punishment by fire is more effective than any other form of punishment. It is no accident that it has been adopted by religion as a lasting punishment for the wicked in the world to come.

Temporary punishment by fire provides guidance and deliverance from eternal, everlasting punishment!

That was what my father meant when he branded me. When I didn't read, and when I continued to tell him that I couldn't read this handwriting –

He branded me!

He branded me in just the way Sadiq would have branded his son, if he had had a son, and if his son had been like me.

He put the red-hot rod on my fingers, then immediately took it off.

On my index finger.

It touched me for just a fraction of a moment, but it had a deadly effect. I cried out. He had closed the door and the window overlooking the street. Then he put the rod on my thumb for a moment. I smelled the smell of flesh – my flesh – and I screamed louder. As he went on with the punishment, he scolded me, telling me to be quiet.

Why then did my mother go out, leaving me to put up with my father's temper on my own, with all the pain and humiliation that brought?

I know.

I know why my mother ran away. I, from whom nothing is hidden.

She ran away to lessen the length of my punishment. If she had stayed, she would have had to stand up to him, and he would have taken his time, in order to challenge and provoke her. She chose the least painful solution, for me and for her.

Before the neighbours arrived, my father put the rod back in its place, put out the light, untied me and went off to open the door. He left without saying a word.

Sadiq was not among them.

My mother came in behind the others but reached me first. She was angry. Her face was dark and flushed, and her neck even more so. She walked around for a bit, backwards and forwards in a confused way. Then she made a beeline for the geography book, grabbed it and took it out of the house. After a few moments, she came back in without it.

I wasn't in any position to protest at what my mother had done, for the neighbours were all around me with their attention focused on my injuries, and I was exhausted and unable to do anything for myself. I was trying unsuccessfully to conquer my tears, but I couldn't stop them flowing.

My mother stayed some distance away from me, leaving the others to attend to my burned fingers. But a blazing argument was raging between us in our heads. I had once asked the employee's son whether his father beat him and he said no. I asked him whether his father told him off, and he said no, only occasionally. I envied him for that. But despite everything, I never wished my mother had married anyone else besides my father. I also asked my friend the employee's son once whether his father knew that the earth was round and that it rotated. He said his father had told him that even before he learned it in school. And his mother? He said that she made fun of them when she heard the two of them talking about the subject.

I hesitated a long time before asking him once if he had told his father that my mother used to kiss him when he came to our house. He was surprised by the question, and I was embarrassed, and the subject was never mentioned between us again.

For many years after that, I continued to surprise myself sometimes wondering whether he still remembered my question to him. The day my mother told me about the circumstances of her marriage, I begged her not to tell anyone, but she replied that today she regarded my brothers and myself as more precious than all the treasures of the earth. I felt a deep contentment: we were in the house at the time, and in front of her was a washing bowl, full of clean, gossamery clothes, brimming over with purity and the warmth of the sun. My mother continued to collect her washing from the roof. She folded the white underwear and put it in the cupboard. She was sitting down. The shadow was magnificent.

But it seems that happiness, Mr Kawabata, is usually tinged with sorrow. It suddenly occurred to me to ask her why she kissed my friend, when his mother did not kiss me. This distressed me. His mother didn't pay me any attention, either when I went into her house or when I left. She treated me like a nobody, neither a plus nor a minus, with complete indifference. Just like my father with her son.

My father.

I can almost see his face as he put the red-hot rod on my finger. He felt pain, I am certain of that.

Abraham also felt pain as he almost plunged the knife into his son's neck, before hearing the voice of God calling him at the decisive moment.

Only fire purifies. Punishment by fire has a deeper effect than any other punishment. It is not by chance, then, that religion has chosen it for the wicked to rest in for ever.

In those days, Mr Kawabata, fire was linked to iron, so that people would say: 'Fire and iron.'

Is fire stronger, or fire and iron?

I forgot everything when my mother showed her love for my father. I felt at ease to the very depth of my soul. But she didn't voice her love explicitly. My mother was not good at expressing herself.

My mother was a tree.

The tree gives of its fruit at the due time. Didn't I tell you, Mr Kawabata, how she answered anyone who commented on how many children she had? She replied that she couldn't keep her children in her stomach at will, even if she had wanted to.

Contrary to what people say about their childhood traumas – in particular, about being shocked when they surprise their parents naked somewhere, or in the same bed (*our people, Mr Kawabata, didn't used to sleep in one bed*) – contrary to what everyone else says, I was happy.

I don't deny that I was surprised, even disturbed, by my parents' behaviour, but it was a disturbance that was born of the moment and disappeared as fast as it came.

I was happy, and this happiness continued to increase with time. My mother loved my father, then. For an embrace, in my eyes (what an embrace!), was an expression of love. As soon as it was daylight, I had made for the bathroom, and they were standing there in a state like nothing on earth. Strange.

As time went on, I built a whole series of analyses on what I had seen. What they were doing that day, they always did, no doubt. By that stage I had begun to learn from my friends the big difference between a man and a woman. I had begun to learn that a man has one hole while a woman has two: one at the back like a man, and another at the front, through which the child emerges after being carried in her womb for nine months. It was a narrow hole, and so the woman suffered a lot of pain when she gave birth. A narrow opening, not even big enough for the finger of a hefty man, so that it hurt a lot when her husband penetrated her, especially for the first time. She would scream and cry, and try to go back home. Many new brides deserted their husbands on their wedding night, and returned to their family home, but their families would force them to return to their husbands, and they would spend weeks and months crying from pain and despair, until they got used to it. Some of them felt a burning sensation, because a man's 'thing' sometimes burned when it touched them somewhere. But their own 'things' got wider and darker with repeated use, so they no longer felt pain.

The man would penetrate the woman, who was crying with fear and embarrassment. She would feel pain, and he would drop into her a fluid, shouting like an animal on heat. So she would become pregnant. Then he would get off her, and she would wrap herself in anything to hand, doubling up in her pain and stifling her groans, while he got up and ate a slice of bread coated with a little sugar.

*'Isn't there any other way?' I asked my friends once.*

Certainly, I understood the meaning of what I was seeing, and my heart was at peace, despite everything that my friends told me.

What reassured me in particular was my knowledge of my mother. If she didn't want something, nobody in the world could force it on her.

Least of all, my father.

He couldn't stop her from going to church barefoot in the rain when the path was soaked with water. That was the day for fulfilling her vows. He simply asked her to wait until the sky brightened up.

'It might rain for a month without stopping,' she shouted at him.

She went and came back. How I wanted to go with her!

I prayed that her foot wouldn't get cut by a piece of glass or a nail lying on the path. I prayed that she wouldn't catch a cold. I waited several days watching for the first symptoms, but they didn't appear. I was afraid that my father would gloat if they did.

When she came back from church that day, it was still raining and bitterly cold. Snow had fallen halfway down the mountains, the peaks were covered and the village streets were deserted.

My mother was drenched, for the church was five minutes away or more, and another five back. The water was dripping from her long hair, and her clothes looked as though they had just been taken out of the washing tub. She heated some water and took it into the bathroom, where she disappeared to wash.

My father went up to the door of the bathroom, which was shut, and bent his head down like someone who has asked a question and is waiting for a reply from the other side of the door. But there was no question, and no reply.

Then she came out of the bathroom, with a towel wrapped around her hair. She was wearing thick, warm clothes. She went up to the heater and sat down beside it. After she had warmed up a little, looking at the red charcoal – my father was meanwhile standing silently beside the window – she asked my sister to comb her hair.

Like a queen. As if my sister was her lady-in-waiting.

At lunchtime, the two of them spoke – my father and mother, that is.

I had been waiting for that moment patiently but anxiously.

My father asked her for a second time about the motive for her vow. (The first time had been before she went to church.) She replied nervously, with a mocking tone that suggested that many things at home were in need of a vow, then asked in the same tone: 'Do you think we're not in need of anything?'

I well remember, Mr Kawabata, I who never forget, that this happened at the beginning of December, and that it was raining for the first time that year.

That year, the trees didn't bear any olives worth speaking of. The quantity we harvested from our olive grove was quite insufficient and the few olives that there were, were shrunken and had no oil in them, because the rain had come so late.

Problems and troubles, and the jars almost empty. It was beyond my mother's capacity to imagine that we could be forced to buy olive oil, when in a good year we would usually be selling it. Impossible!

Security resided in a steady job.

It was around that time that the employee's wife was in hospital, having her second child there, because the state paid all her expenses. My mother, like the other women of the quarter, used to go to do his house-keeping in the absence of his wife. The men of the quarter didn't leave him alone either. My father would go with my mother, and I would go with them. On one occasion, however, I went just with my mother. She hadn't asked me to, I just saw her going out of the house, so I joined her. She saw me walking with her but didn't comment. I knew full well where she was going. She went in and so did I. He welcomed her and thanked her. She headed straight for the kitchen, so I followed her and stayed with her, not venturing out for a moment. Occasionally he would come in to ask her if she needed anything. Every time he came in I would look at him as if I were seeing him for the first time. He was like someone who lived in the city. He was as pale as they were, his flesh was soft, and he was clean – clean under the fingernails, as my mother used to say about people with steady jobs – but his cleanliness was not the cleanliness of a man who sweated, or whose body and clothes were used to the feel of earth.

I didn't exactly feel loathing towards him, but I wouldn't have chosen him as my husband if I'd been a woman.

He was wearing a necktie, and the top of the knot was covered by the flesh of his neck. Some words he pronounced like a city-dweller.

The whole time that I spent with my mother in the kitchen, I was preparing myself for the moment when she would ask me to go home to get her something.

I would certainly refuse. But...

I was afraid of refusing in too provocative a way – of saying, for example, before she'd asked me anything: 'I won't leave this place.'

But my mother never asked me anything at all.

Then one of the neighbours came, followed by several other visitors. My mother handed over the work and went back home. As I was leaving with my mother, I asked the man about his son, and he said that he was with his mother, who'd wanted to see him.

I often wondered later, Mr Kawabata, what I would have done if my mother had pressed me (as she often used to press me) and screamed in my face, and hit me with one of her shoes as I ran away from her. But would I have run away from her?

That night, Mr Kawabata, I said my prayers. It wasn't thanks that drove me to pray, but fear.

Fear.

I mean, as when lightning, for example, strikes a church steeple, as if to provoke the mighty Creator of the universe.

I haven't forgotten to tell you, Mr Kawabata, that some time after the neighbour's arrival, my mother asked her to bring a frying-pan for her from our house. This request provoked my questions rather than satisfying them.

I haven't forgotten to tell you that, I was simply waiting. *Mr Kawabata, I've already told you that I sometimes use certain expressions that I might describe as 'fundamental'. Here is one of them:*

*'If everyone revealed what was in his heart, the whole earth would smell unbearably.'*

I wasn't able to formulate at the time what had happened, as I did afterwards. After I'd moved up in school, I began to tell myself that before the neighbour had come, my mother had wanted to ask me to do what she asked her neighbour to do, but she didn't dare. Or didn't have the will to.

*Ah, trees, you bear fruit when the fruit comes to you.*

When she asked the woman, it was as though she had lanced a boil full of pus. And found relief. She had poured out everything in her heart.

When she came back home, and I with her, my father asked her in an ordinary voice (no one could doubt that it was an ordinary voice): 'Where have you been?' So she told him.

I was nervous in case he asked me whether I was with her, or whether I'd gone away and hidden. But where could I go away to, where could I hide in this one-room house?

Anyway, I didn't really want to go away. I wanted to stay here watching what was going on, because the matter concerned me more than anyone else.

'Do you believe that we will be forced to buy oil this year?'

'How can we avoid it? Don't you think we must?'

I knew that Sadiq would tell my father about our meetings that everyone in town had heard about, but I was certain that he wouldn't tell him about the incident with the newspaper. This was for two reasons. The first was the nature of what had happened between us, which was so cruel and painful that modesty required that we pretend not to have noticed it and make sure never to talk about it. The second was that my father would not allow anyone else to beat me. This was something that was well known, and well known to Sadiq in particular. My father almost stabbed the son of one of Sadiq's relatives with a knife because he'd hit me while we were playing on a piece of wasteland in the quarter. I'd only just finished complaining to my father on that occasion, when he grabbed a knife and rushed off to the wasteground, heading straight for the boy. The boy, who was older than me, saw him charging towards him and ran away, but my father carried on chasing him until he caught him up. He was about to stab him but the boy cried out for help, so my father abandoned the knife, and started hitting him on the head with his hand and kicking him until he had properly beaten him up.

'You've sent my son back to me like a plucked chicken!' the boy's mother screamed in my father's face. 'Wait until his father comes back!' she added, threateningly.

When his father did come back, his wife didn't let him cross the threshold, but told him everything that had happened while he was still some yards away. He had a shovel in his hands, which he lifted before reaching my father, intending to bring it down on him. But my father was alert and expecting this reaction, so he wasn't surprised by it. He was able to avoid the blow by dodging out of the way, so that the shovel came down on the asphalt of the road, making the sparks fly. My father then forestalled him – his revolver was on his hip, but he preferred to use the knife – and managed to deal him a blow (fortunately, a superficial one) on the hip. *I say fortunately, Mr Kawabata, because I didn't want him to kill him, even though I was happy that he had scored a decisive point over him!* At that point, the neighbours intervened and were able to separate the two of them.

People were not able to separate my mother and the neighbour's wife, however – they weren't locked in a physical struggle but were hurling abuse at each other from a distance of several metres.

This was the first time I had heard my mother using language like that – the sort of language that my friends and I later used to whisper to one another, albeit in a different way and for a different purpose.

'Cock-sucker...!' screamed my mother.

'Cock-sucker yourself...you whore!' the neighbour shouted back.

My mother replied with an oath which made her leap several feet into the air. 'Me the whore?' shouted my mother. 'Wasn't it you that got pregnant by this monkey' (pointing with her hand at a particular man) 'on the hillside among the olive groves?'

The man in question was standing there with his wife and small children.

The other woman replied that she (my mother, that is) was...and said some things that I couldn't make out, but which struck me as quite shocking and outrageous. I felt I was losing my balance and was about to pass out. Both women were foaming at the mouth with rage.

Finally the neighbours managed to get both of them back into their own houses.

The incident of my beating almost led to a murder. How had Sadiq dared to tell him? Even the teachers in school hesitated for a long time before beating me, and for my part I was very careful not to do anything I deserved to be beaten for, in case one of them beat me and my father found out about it.

I remember once that I was in class about midday, a few moments before the bell rang. I was wanting to go to the toilet more and more, in fact I was quite desperate; but after three pupils had asked permission to go to the toilet one after the other, the schoolmaster had warned us that he had decided to refuse all requests of this kind, and that anyone who dared to ask would get two 'heavyweight' canes on each hand. Unfortunately, the urge came on me suddenly, and instead of stopping within reasonable bounds, got out of control. This schoolmaster was well known for his obstinacy and stubbornness once he had made up his mind. A few seconds (certainly less than a minute) before the bell went, my resistance collapsed. Then the bell sounded before the effects could become too obvious all around me.

At home, I couldn't hide the truth. My father was angry, and went to see the schoolmaster in his house, and they exchanged angry words.

Later, I began to be secretly afraid for the geography teacher. But influencing the geography teacher wasn't easy. His personality was different. He was strong, but he didn't draw his strength from being a member of one of the town's leading families. His strength came from something else – from his different way of approaching people, and from the combination of manners and daring he alone enjoyed.

Sadiq knew all about my father's temperament; in fact, he knew everything about him, as he was his closest friend. It was my father who had arranged his marriage, and it was my father who had acted as a go-between between him and his wife's family when she died two years after their wedding from an illness nobody had been able to diagnose: her appetite had simply faded away until it disappeared altogether, while she became thinner and thinner until she was no more than a skeleton. Then she shut her eyes for ever, without blaming anything or anyone, and before she had had any children. All this in the silence for which she had been known since her marriage.

There is nothing else of interest to be said about Sadiq's married life, except that he would curse human nature after he had finished making love to his wife, with the words: 'Curse this life!'

How had he come to tell him, then?

Or had he simply told him how I'd read the newspaper to him, without telling him that he'd carried on beating me with a thick cane, until there was only just enough of it left to grasp? But Sadiq did not lie. That is something I can be absolutely certain of.

Nobody, certainly not my mother, could have foreseen my father's death as Sadiq foresaw it, despite the fact that no one was actually surprised by the way he died.

Sadiq saw him approaching his end, I am certain of that, for he was closer to him than anyone else – though this closeness didn't necessarily mean that my father confided in him everything in his heart.

Sadiq guessed what actually happened. If he had been summoned to testify concerning the circumstances of his death, and been willing to relate what the eye could not see, he would have accused me without hesitation.

I said that no one was surprised by the way my father

died, but it was still a shocking death as far as I was concerned.

My father knew that I had gone to Beirut with some friends to take part in a demonstration called by the General Workers' Union, and supported by the leftist parties and the other political forces supporting the Palestinian resistance. At that time there was an intimate connection between the rotation of the earth (i.e. scientific fact), the struggle for political demands, and the Palestinian resistance which was aiming to crush the illegal occupiers – the Zionist enemy – and destroy the state they had set up by force on Palestinian soil.

This was the second time I had been to Beirut. The first time was when my father had taken me with him to the airport, when I was no more than ten. But this was the first time that I'd made the decision on my own to go, without the knowledge of my parents and certainly against their will.

My friends and I had been following the difficult negotiations that the workers' representatives were engaged in with the Lebanese government, through the progressive press that we bought every day, morning and evening.

The date of the general strike had been fixed for about a month and time was marching on towards the fateful day.

The workers were demanding wage increases in all sectors. The government's position was that the state's resources would not allow such increases, and the private sector was in the same position.

By that time, we had begun to realize that the government could not act as a referee between the workers and the private-sector employers, because in the final analysis it was the latter that the state represented. At the same time, it couldn't hide behind the state's limited resources, because it was the state that was responsible for squandering those very resources, by turning a blind eye to all sorts of dubious transactions, including the theft of public money. It was also failing to collect taxes on the enormous profits being raked in by capitalist business-men, traders, industrialists and the like.

Moreover – and this is the real crux – a victory of this magnitude won by the working classes would double their self-confidence, and their enormous latent potential, increasing their sense of their historical role and thereby constituting a major step towards achieving power.

In addition to all this (the importance of which will be obvious to everyone), such a victory would have tremendous consequences for the course of the progressive tide generally, and for the credibility of the scientific socialist view as a beacon of the struggle.

Last but not least, such a victory would be a demon-stration of the correctness of collective action, which sprang from our belief in the unity of the shared destiny of the popular forces and masses in Lebanon, and the armed Palestinian resistance located on its territory. Were it not for the existence of this armed Palestinian resistance, with its support for its allies among the progressive Lebanese and Islamic masses, it would have been impossible to force the authorities, as embodied in the Maronite hegemony, to make these concessions.

We used to buy the newspapers, then throw them away after reading them without taking them home. This was to avoid exposing ourselves to questions the answers to which would start a battle with our families – a battle that had been postponed and which it wasn't in our interest to start now. But...

Despite these precautions, my father came across one of these newspapers on the table at home where I used to put my books. He picked it up and started flicking through its pages, looking at those strange faces (those 'creatures', as he used to say when he saw pictures of people whose names were always being mentioned in the newspapers and on the radio), but without understanding anything of what he was seeing. Forced to ask my mother for help, he took the newspaper to her and told her that he was puzzled. My mother couldn't hide her astonishment, which only increased his suspicions.

'Where do you think protecting him and defending him as you do will lead us?' he asked.

'What's the harm in reading a newspaper?' asked my mother, trying to recover from the blow that had struck her.

'Yesterday the earth was a revolving sphere, today there are newspapers, tomorrow God will not exist! Unless you believe that a newspaper is a prayerbook!'

There was a viper in the house!

'There's a viper in the house!' shouted my father in my mother's face angrily. He was not to be contradicted. 'There's a viper in the house. Can you live here?

'And sleep?'

In our country, Mr Kawabata, the viper is a dangerous, poisonous creature, whose danger doesn't just lie in its poison, but in its malice and its ability to creep wherever it likes without your noticing it, however careful you're being.

In our country, Mr Kawabata, it is also a man's right – however brave and fearless he may be – to shudder with fear at the sight of a snake. My father couldn't bear the sight of my mother with her smooth belly after each delivery, for the walls of our house were full of cracks between the stones, which snakes would slip through, creeping into our things and surprising us when we weren't on our guard.

Snakes are afraid of pregnant women and keep away from them, hiding beneath the seventh layer of the earth.

But now my mother was pregnant, and the snake in front of her was not afraid of pregnant women. The methods he'd used before didn't work with this snake. It had no head to be cut off, and it wouldn't be choked by smoke. Spells wouldn't frighten it away, and it couldn't be poisoned. What was to be done, then? He took the newspaper to Bu Mikhail, who read and wrote for the quarter. My mother tried to stop him going, in case he let out some secret that would lead him to some exhausting confrontation with me – *exhausting, in fact, for the whole family, but especially for her.*

'Tear it up, so that he can't read it any more, and that will be the end of it.'

'No,' he said. 'This isn't like the vipers we know, which you can get rid of for ever by killing them. This one needs dealing with in a different way.'

Bu Mikhail took the newspaper from my father and looked at it for some time, under my father's impatient gaze. Then he said that he wouldn't read it to him, because reading it wouldn't do any good. 'I advise you to sort things out quickly if you can't get him to forget. But try to make him forget first!'

'How?' asked my father.

'You know best,' said Bu Mikhail. 'You're the best man of your generation!'

How then could my father, the best man of his generation according to Bu Mikhail's testimony, make me forget?

I remember very well, Mr Kawabata, what happened to me and about me, and I cannot forget it.

What did my father do, then?

My father did nothing. His only option – a decisive confrontation with me, that is – was a very difficult matter. Adopting this option would lead to the break-up of the whole family. If the family broke up he would not be able to continue as a normal person, one of the sons of this old-established village, the master of one of its households and one of its blessed and valiant heroes – my father. So he was silent.

My father never mentioned the newspaper. Not only that, he even put it back in its place on the table where it had been before, just as it was. It was open at the same page and the same article, so that when I returned home I could never have guessed that anything had been altered, or realized that anything had happened during my absence. It was only my mother who told me everything. My mother told me that if I went on like this I would destroy the house. 'Listen,' I said, 'it was only a few years ago that you used to go down to the river carrying our dirty clothes to wash them there. Now there's water inside the house, and you only have to turn on a tap, and water gushes from it like a waterfall. An even shorter time ago, your nights were dark, but now all you have to do is to press a small switch fixed to the wall for night to be turned into day. How many times have you said to my father that one day we should think of buying a refrigerator, so that we can get rid of this food cage that hangs by a cord from the ceiling in the middle of the house?' *It was impossible for me to remind her of her happiness when my father sent one of us to bring ice-cold water from our neighbour's fridge – the neighbour with a steady job – and sometimes even actual ice, ice like that on the mountain-tops, if not harder.* I also asked her: 'Do you know where this gas comes from? The gas which you've been cooking on for just a few months, cooking whatever you like without any noise or bother, lighting it just once with a single match?

'It's science,' I said to her.

'It's science that has made it possible for you (you and he, that is) to have six children so far, and for all of them to stay alive. Not a single one has died! It's the same science that can see with its own eyes, as you see with your eyes, that the earth is a sphere and that it rotates. What's wrong with science, what fault is it of science's, if it sees as you see? You can see with your own eyes that the refrigerator keeps food cold, and turns water into ice. In the same way, science sees that the earth is a sphere and that it rotates!'

So she answered me.

Yes, for the first time my mother actually answered me!

She'd usually been content just to advise me, but now she confronted me with the argument that I had to get my Higher Certificate (she'd begun to describe the certificate I'd get as the 'Higher Certificate' ever since I started secondary school) so that I could get the best job and the best wife possible.

'Where do you get these ideas from?' she said. 'I've never heard of any community or religion that believes in the things you claim. Which book are you and your friends reading? – those friends that you never stop hanging around night or day. Listen, my son. Drive out these wicked thoughts from your heart. We are people who need God to give us a recompense for our suffering.'

At this point . . .

At this point I could stand no more, especially as I was still finishing reading Brecht's play about the life of the famous astronomer Galileo. I was still discussing it with my friends, with a pleasure and enthusiasm that I hadn't known before. So I answered with the words of Galileo in the play – namely, that there is no reward to be collected in heaven for the suffering you suffer today.

'Shut up!' said my mother. Yes, she had scolded me!

My gentle mother, my mother the tree, had scolded me!

It was a long time since she'd scolded me, many years in fact. She hadn't done so since I'd passed my first certificate. After that, her respect for me had begun to increase. I had easily passed the Intermediate Certificate, and now I was on the threshold of a very important examination – the Baccalaureate. There weren't many people in the village who had passed it, and it was the door to very, very high-up positions. My mother was proud of me and liked to talk about me, and she liked it when the other women praised me to make her happy.

My mother told me to shut up, then went on: 'So we spend our lives on a pebble, then, on a pebble turning among other pebbles, too many to be counted, in an infinite universe! What's got into that fine brain of yours? We're a round object lost among a lot of other round objects, lost in the universe! Have some sense! So we're not under God's eyes now?'

I'd never enjoyed hearing my mother speak as much as I did on that occasion, and I'd never felt such great happiness.

Mr Kawabata,

I saw, in a tangible way, how the books were right!

In a tangible way!

For what my mother was saying (my mother, who'd

never read a word in her life) was exactly what the young monk was saying when he addressed Galileo in the Florentine ambassador's palace. Listen to the young monk's words: 'I am from a peasant family, from simple folk who know everything about olive trees, but apart from that nothing worth mentioning. When I set out to observe the phases that the planet Venus passes through' – *the monk is also an astronomer, who has decided to give up science, for fear of the dangerous consequences that may result from his discoveries* – 'I imagine I can see my parents and my sister huddled around the fire, eating their humble supper under roofbeams blackened by smoke over the years. I imagine their hands worn out by time, I see them in all their detail, I see the spoon between their coarse fingers. Their life is not a happy one. But in the midst of this very misery of theirs, there is a certain principle of order. What would they say if they heard me repeating to them that they were living on a small pebble, which revolved continuously in empty space around another body? A pebble among many pebbles without any special significance! What use would anything be to them after that?

'What would have been the point of all this patience, then, of this acceptance of misery, of this acceptance of sweat and hunger and humiliation?

'No!

'If you spoke to them like this, their eyes would start out of their sockets, and the crumbs that they were carrying to their mouths would fall from their hands. They would stare at me as if to say: "So we've been that stupid all our lives! The eyes of our Lord, then, are not directed at us! No one has given us any special role or meaning! There is nothing but misery, then, on this small planet which no one has given any special meaning. This hunger is simply a form of deprivation and lack of possessions; it is not a trial set by God, to test our will and love and obedience."'

Mr Kawabata, aren't you persuaded, like me, that this is exactly what my mother meant, indeed that this was what she said explicitly – despite the fact that she was illiterate and incapable of deciphering a single letter? Who could have taught her to speak like this? Could it have been the local priest, do you suppose? But there was no priest in the village with a Higher Certificate.

I asked her without a moment's hesitation, slightly mockingly (no, very mockingly): 'Who taught you to speak like this?'

The fact is, Mr Kawabata, that when I heard what she was saying, I couldn't believe it was coming from her mouth.

She answered, also without a moment's hesitation, that nobody needed to learn to see the face of God. Even the dumb chicken raises its head in thanks to God while drinking. 'I have never heard anyone, man or jinn, utter poisoned words like these – Christian, Muslim, Jew, even a fire-worshipper!'

At that time I knew nothing whatever about Islam. I hadn't yet met comrade Hasan at the University of Beirut, who told me about the exhausting confrontation between himself and his father the sheikh over the fact that the earth was round and rotated. He told me that his father was cleverer than my mother, in the first place because he could read and write well, and secondly because he read the newspaper from time to time. It was for this reason that his father had retreated quickly in the face of the first attack from his son Hasan, after Gagarin had made his famous orbit of the earth, and conceded to him that the earth was round and rotated. His retreat, however, was not a surrender, but rather part of a studied plan to avoid defeat, for he had constructed for himself a second line of defence. *Hasan always used to use these battlefield expressions in all his conversations, even in his accounts of his amorous adventures.* He started by saying that the state of the earth as revealed by modern science had been stipulated in the Qur'an, and that for this reason it was in no way in contradiction to its teachings. This made Hasan angry. He set about looking in the Qur'an for the verses mentioning heaven and earth, which he considered stated with absolute certainty that God had spread out the earth and levelled it, that he had built the heavens over it, that the stars were lamps suspended in the heavens, and so on. He collected them all together in one list, with the name of the *sura*, the verse and page number, and confronted his father with them.

'And where did all this lead, Hasan?'

Hasan replied that in the end it had led to his leaving his home and his village and to his taking up permanent residence in Beirut!

'Aren't you the same today?'

'No,' he said. 'The situation today has changed fundamentally. The battle raging now is with the Zionist enemy and the Lebanese regime.' *We were then at the beginning of the seventies, and the armed Palestinian resistance was at its height, strongly supported by the Sunni Muslims, and of course by the leftist parties.* 'Unlike most others of his sect, my father the sheikh was by nature and intellect opposed to injustice and oppression, and certainly opposed to Israel. So we glossed over our differences and closed the book on our metaphysical disagreements. And you?' asked Hasan. 'How have things worked out with you?' 'They ended in the death of my father,' I replied. 'So it was fate that settled things between the two of you,' he said. 'We could say that, if we wanted.' 'And if we didn't want to say that, what then?' he asked. 'Then the matter would become very complicated,' I replied. 'Enlighten me, sir!' he said. *Hasan used to like to use these eloquent, old-fashioned expressions, which I thought probably represented a fond recollection of the words of his father the sheikh, his ally.* 'It might be a long story,' I said. 'So be it,' he said. 'Or do you believe that we Arabs have no time?' I smiled. I smiled because I knew his theory of time – he called it the theory of 'connecting vessels' – which stated that those peoples that had time lacked everything else. 'Is it such a complicated story?' he asked. 'Is it so difficult for you to tell it?' 'My father was killed, like many others like him,' I said, 'for reasons connected with a family feud.' 'What's so strange about that?' he said. 'In that northern Maronite village of yours, you are known for your feuds and family vendettas. That is one of the central planks of your struggle there.' 'I wish it were all as simple as that,' I said. 'The problem is with me. I cannot think of my father's death without linking it to relations between the two of us. Our relationship was one of remorseless war. He saw me drifting from the rotation of the earth to atheism, from there to socialism, and from there to the Palestinian resistance – all of which he believed were opposed to the Lebanese state that the Christians had been able to establish with the help of France. True, they'd established an authority which they shared with the Islamic factions, but they'd kept the final say within it for themselves, thus safeguarding themselves against a return to the previous situation under which they'd been a protected minority under Muslim domination for a period of more than thirteen hundred years. The sad thing was that, not being the type of person to reveal what was in his heart, he never spoke about the matter. He would say nothing for ages, then suddenly explode. Naturally, I wasn't able to take the initiative to broach the subject with him. I wish I'd been able to say to him that we weren't aiming to give the Muslims power over the Christians through our struggle. On the contrary, we wanted to overturn this regime and replace it with another regime that would establish justice and equality among men, and deal with the individual on the basis of common citizenship, not sectarian or family allegiance. Only a regime like that could guarantee people's freedom of belief and expression and employment, not to speak of their culture, recreation, leisure and medical treatment. This was what socialism was. The Palestinians had a sacred right to return to their homeland (this was an idea he supported; what he feared was that they would come pouring into Lebanon from every other Arab country and form an alliance with the Muslims – the other countries may have denied them arms while they were there, but they would arm them and support them in every possible way when they arrived in Lebanon), and it was our duty to help them, because their enemy was also our enemy. I wish I had been able to say that!'

'And what has all that got to do with his death?'

The fact is that I found it really difficult to express the connection between the two things sensibly. But I could never think of his death without linking it to relations between us. I was almost certain that no one in this universe had ever experienced his father as I did mine. After the incident of the newspaper, he no longer spoke to me at all, and he even started to avoid the house when I was in it.

'It's ignorance,' said Hasan. His own father, he continued, used to rip up his French schoolbooks in case they corrupted his pure Muslim mind with the filth and immorality and unbelief that they contained. Several times he had blocked the path of pupils going to school in the next village and ripped up their French books. This created a division among the families, some of whom supported him and some of whom were opposed. When things settled down, families were left with the freedom to choose whatever they thought appropriate for the future of their children. He also said that if it hadn't been for his mother, he wouldn't have been able to continue his studies at school – though his mother hadn't succeeded in sending his sisters to school. 'When my friends and I headed for Beirut to take part in the demonstration,' I said, 'his bewilderment reached the point of madness, and he maintained his silence for an amazing length of time. If you'd made his acquaintance during that period, you'd have said that he was silence incarnate in a human frame. And naturally, his silence was linked to anger and vexation.'

Our plan was that no one should know we had gone, especially our families. But a ship cannot always choose its own wind, so to speak, and chance dictated that things should not turn out quite as we intended.

We arrived very early at Burj Square, the place that had been designated as the starting-point of the demonstration. It was about ten o'clock, and the time of the demonstration had been set for three in the afternoon.

We didn't pay much attention, while we were re-hearsing the plan, to how we were to spend the time between our arrival and the time set for the demonstration. What we were thinking about was how to escape from both school and home without attracting anyone's attention, and how to return from Beirut when the demonstration finished just before sunset, when lessons in school finished at four in the afternoon.

The first problem was not particularly difficult to solve, because we knew all the tricks involved in playing truant from home or school. It was the problem of how to get back home late in the day that needed a fertile imagination. We decided, therefore, to attend only the start of the demonstration, and to go back to our village immediately afterwards. We would certainly reach home before six, and we might arrive before five, or around four-thirty, if we were lucky enough to find a fast driver – especially as there were five of us (a full load), so that the driver could start immediately without waiting for more passengers.

We arrived in Beirut, then, with a long time in front of us – five hours, which we didn't know how to spend. We talked about it at length as we walked round the areas next to the square. We couldn't go too far away from the square in case we got lost, but at the same time we had to avoid waiting there, and especially avoid going too near to the pick-up point for taxis taking passengers between Beirut and our village. Otherwise, we might meet someone we knew from the village and fall into a trap we dare not fall into at all costs.

Quite by chance, as we wandered round these streets, we found ourselves in the red-light district. Its official name was Mutanabbi Street. This Mutanabbi, being one of the most famous and important classical Arab poets, was the very poet that we were studying that year in our Arabic literature classes for the Baccalaureate. We laughed loud and long, but we quickly became serious again, as we concluded from this superficially un-important coincidence that the state was negligent (state negligence: that was an expression we were always using, Mr Kawabata), and that it attached no importance to literature or writers, let alone to science and scientists, or ideas and intellectuals!

We started to wander round and round, finding ourselves in this same street time and again. We started to read the signs with women's names written on them. Marika! This name caught our attention. It wasn't yet noon. We were struck by the fact that the signs were no different from other signs belonging to shops, cafés and other similar establishments! We were struck by the women we saw coming out of the buildings and going into the shops next door to buy things. We were struck by a whole lot of things. Why shouldn't we go in to one of the buildings? Why shouldn't we try it? We discussed the matter and the majority view was in favour, so we did.

We went in through the door of a building into a passage that was dark compared with the daylight outside. Then we went up a staircase until we reached an open door, where we stood waiting, hesitantly, uncertain what we were supposed to do. Should we go in, or should we call out? Should we wait until someone appeared, or should we go away? An elderly man of around sixty, wearing socks but no shoes, looked out, came towards us and asked us what we wanted. We were taken aback by this question. Indeed, we might have expected almost anything except this question – like a shopkeeper asking you, for example, in surprise: 'Why have you come into my shop?' We were lost for a reply, and our confusion was doubtless apparent on our faces, which had turned a definite red. We looked at each other and started to back out, as if by an unspoken agreement, but he stopped us in our tracks, saying: 'Do you want to come in?' We nodded our heads, to indicate that this was exactly what we did want. 'Do you really know where you are?' he asked. 'Of course,' we told him. 'Come in, then,' he said, sitting us down in what was presumably a waiting room, as he disappeared into one of the other rooms. He was away for several minutes at least, during which time we all tried to cope with our embarrassment and stop our pulses racing. Then we heard a sudden shout and heard the voice of a woman saying: 'Let me sleep! Who are these people with hard-ons before dawn? So what if there are a thousand of them! Leave me alone,' she went on, 'I want to sleep. Do you think I'm a machine?' We immediately beat a retreat, without thinking about it, and in a moment were on the pavement in the street below, desperately trying to get away from the place as quickly as possible. It was still only around midday so we went to eat *falafel*. This was the first time we'd eaten this dish, though we'd often heard about it. We stared in amazement at the speed of the man's hands making the sandwiches. It was still very early for the time of the demonstration, so we started wandering again through the nearby streets, only to find ourselves once again in the red-light district, Mutanabbi Street. This time we stopped by a different sign, with the name of a different woman written on it. We went in. There was an elderly woman in the reception room, more than sixty years old. She welcomed us in a way that put us at our ease and immediately told us that it was still rather early for what we wanted, but she would try to find us at least 'one' who was ready. She went away for a few minutes, then came back with two women about forty years old, still in their nightclothes. One of them started talking to us immediately, without even bothering to say hello, saying something that we didn't understand at first, we were so surprised by her tone of voice and accent, and manner of speaking. But we understood everything when she added: 'If you don't want to do that, the lady' (pointing to the lady who had welcomed us) 'will make you come under her armpit for a quarter of a lira each.' It wasn't difficult for us to do a quick mental calculation, and for each of us to understand that if he paid three lira, he wouldn't have enough left to return home, so we had no choice but to agree or to go away.

As we began to waver, she noticed our hesitation. 'Can't you pay that much?' she asked. We remained silent, not a single one of us saying anything, while she looked at us with just a trace of a smile beginning to appear on her face. She saw that we were still silent and embarrassed. 'Decide among yourselves quickly how much you can pay,' she said, 'and tell the lady.' Then she turned her back on us and quickly went off back where she'd come from, with her friend following her, while we turned towards each other and began making some quick, drastic calculations. Only one of us said he'd do it with the old woman. He said that this in itself would be the 'experience of a lifetime' (it was this expression – 'the experience of a lifetime' – that had tipped the balance in favour of the enterprise while we were discussing it with her). The other four of us decided that we could pay eight liras maximum. We gave our decision to the lady, who was waiting for us patiently in silence, and she slowly got up to tell the two women. After a few moments she returned to lead us inside, and we found ourselves in a room with two beds in it, one woman on each bed. They were stretched out with their bottoms completely naked. The sight was something that almost made one want to turn one's face away. They hurried us on to pay first, then take our clothes off, and for each of us to take his turn. We did as we were told, paid and hurried up. We only got a few seconds' sex each, except for the last of us, who was having difficulty coming, in spite of the fact that he was trying to as hard as he could. When she told him to hurry up, he started trying even harder, but still without success. Then she told him off and said that she could have fucked a whole town in the time. This sort of atmosphere wasn't making things any easier for him, but he insisted on finishing, though torrents of sweat were pouring from his body. Suddenly she sprang up and pushed him off her, almost throwing him off the bed on to the floor. Our friend, however, also jumped up this time. 'Give me back my money!' he shouted. 'You're treating me like a machine!' At this point the rest of us intervened to stop a fight between them, and after some toing and froing we agreed to pay her another lira if she let him finish his turn when we'd all gone out and left them alone in the room.

In the reception room, where we'd gone to wait, we failed to find our friend who'd chosen the armpit job. The old woman told us that he was waiting for us downstairs at the entrance to the building. After a short while – no longer than two or three minutes at the very most – our other friend came back from the room where we'd left him, still doing up his clothes and wiping the beads of sweat from his face and neck.

We came out of the building into full view on the pavement but we still didn't find our friend. We were alarmed and spent several minutes looking for him everywhere, consumed by fear, nervousness and uncertainty. Finally, with a great sense of relief, we saw him waving his hand at us from a distance, beckoning us to join him. We were still some paces away when he told us that someone from the village had seen him coming out of the building and asked him what he was doing there, upstairs. He hadn't given a reply. We were all dumbfounded. After discussion, however, we recovered from the blow, as we realized that the damage, if there was any, would be partial rather than total, since even in the worst possible case our friend would be the only victim. The rest of us would all escape and the purpose behind our visit to Beirut would remain a closely guarded secret.

Then again, in all likelihood the man wouldn't tell anyone else what he'd seen, because that wouldn't be in his own interest. After all, it would be logical, in the event that he told on *us*, that he should also be quizzed about the reason for *his* being there!

Anyway, now that what had happened had happened – which was something we couldn't change at all – the only thing for us to do was to forget the incident and wait for whatever might happen. So we decided to forget it and to continue our 'excursion' until the time for the start of the demonstration.

It was still early, only just after one o'clock. The overwhelming happiness that we felt at participating in events shaping the future was mingled with a feeling of apprehension that we could not completely suppress.

Then events began to gather speed and to occupy all our interest and attention. More and more shops started closing, one after the other, and we started to see groups of people marching together with banners waving and slogans held aloft.

By two o'clock almost all the shops had shut. People had gathered in the square, and the crowds were growing thicker and thicker. There were banners, with slogans on them against the capitalist clique and oppressive regime. Some of them called for the state to open the borders with Israel to the Palestinian guerrillas. Others called on the working class to revolt, to change the regime and to build socialism. A lone banner which caught our particular attention demanded the presidency of the republic for the Muslims. We secretly hoped that no one from our village would see it and wondered how the people carrying it could be allowed to participate in this progressive demonstration. Shouts began to ring out from groups of people scattered in various parts of the square. Each group formed a circle around someone who led the chanting, with those around him either repeating what he said, or answering him with carefully rehearsed slogans.

Three o'clock came. We waited for the demonstration to set off, so that we could walk in it for a little before beginning the next stage – the journey back to our village. Another quarter of an hour went by, and it had not yet moved. Then another quarter of an hour went by, without any apparent indication that the demonstration had either begun to move, or that it was about to do so. What was happening, then? Why this delay? Nobody we asked could tell us anything. One person, who seemed to be among the organizers of the demonstration – the bride's mother, so to speak – laughed at our question and our obvious anxiety, asking us: 'Do you have something that is more important than the struggle on your minds?' We told him where we'd come from, and where we had to get back to, and that we'd come without our families' knowledge. He appeared surprised, expressing great admiration for our courage, and great appreciation for our stand. We were absolutely delighted, as if we had taken a step into paradise, and we resolved to stay and take part in the demonstration until the end, however much it cost us. A moment's reflection, however, brought us back to our senses, and the necessity of making a move and heading back immediately. The path of the struggle was long, and we were still at the beginning of it.

We hadn't made allowances in our plans for the fact that Martyrs' Square would empty of taxis when the demonstrators started to march!

Nor had we taken note of where we would then be able to find a taxi to get us back to our village!

So we found ourselves in the middle of the trap we had worked for so long to avoid falling into! We started looking unsuccessfully for a taxi in the nearby streets – the same streets that we were trying not to get too far away from, in case we got lost. But all we came across were nervous policemen, whom we couldn't ask anything because they were the arm of the law, and if they knew the motives for our presence there, they wouldn't treat us gently.

The solution?

We had two options. Either go back to the demonstration until it finished, then carry on wandering around all night until daybreak, when the village taxis would return to their stands in Martyrs' Square; or else leave the square and find an ordinary taxi for which we would have to pay a return fare. The second option, however, would require a greater sum of money than we possessed – and we would certainly have to pay it in full if we did decide to go back immediately, however difficult that might be.

Everyone back home knew that a man from our village ran a small hotel in Burj Square. It was no more than a single storey in an old building where the Ahdab buses stood. These were the buses that carried passengers between Beirut and Tripoli – in fact, we'd come in one of them. So we went back there, in the hope of borrowing the money we needed from him. It was five o'clock and the square was completely empty of people and cars, with only a few policemen wandering around or standing at the road junctions.

We crossed over and went up to the second floor, where the hotel was. We didn't find the owner, but we did find a member of staff from our village, as well as some hotel residents, who recognized us from the fact that our faces bore a family resemblance. We told them that we were in our Baccalaureate year and that we'd come to Beirut to submit official examination applications.

When I arrived home I spoke to my mother, while my father stood listening without saying a word. The time was a little after half past seven. I simply told her what we'd agreed between ourselves, as friends, we should say – that we'd gone to Beirut because we needed to know the date of the examinations, to submit our applications and so on. But as soon as I told her that we'd been forced to borrow money as we were too late to find a taxi from the village in Burj Square because of the demonstration, my father immediately left the house.

That night was one of those rare nights when I slept in my bed while my father's bed remained empty.

I couldn't sleep until he had come back, well into the night. My mother got up to meet him but he didn't reply to her many questions. He contented himself with a few brief words to the effect that everything had gone all right, then slipped under the blanket on his bed and went to sleep.

When my father heard what I'd said to my mother,

he'd immediately gone to the house of a taxi-driver who lived close to us and asked him to take him to Beirut, where he went to the hotel, paid the debt that I owed and came back again.

Naturally, he paid the fare there and back!

This was a period of parliamentary elections in Lebanon, and the atmosphere between the five leading families was electric. They were competing for three seats allocated to our parliamentary constituency, which was made up of our own village, and the other smaller villages of the district, which had a Maronite majority population.

My father was always an enthusiastic campaigner for the family to which we gave our allegiance, but on this occasion his enthusiasm was of a different order – stronger and more committed than usual. On the result of this struggle important things might depend (*was this really the reason for his unusual enthusiasm, when so many important elections had been held before?*), since the head of our family who was a candidate for election enjoyed a widespread reputation among the Christians generally, and his election as president of the republic was a real possibility if he won. The regime's interests needed a strong man to take on the Palestinian, leftist, Sunni Muslim alliance, and our village was well known for the courage and fortitude of its men, who could forget their differences and stand together at decisive moments, especially when their country was in danger. At this point the family received information that some members of an opposing family were threatening our supporters in one of the villages. Among the names mentioned was that of the watchman who had deceived my father, and who'd given him the beating that had hurt him 'psychologically rather than physically'. So my father

97

enlisted with the others to return the insult. The two groups met and exchanged abuse, sensible men intervened, but the affair dragged on for several days, with arguments, counter-arguments and various provocations, and without any mediator succeeding in defusing the situation, until my father ambushed the watchman and killed him; having killed him, he took his revolver.

That year I succeeded in passing my Baccalaureate examinations at the first attempt, despite all these problems and pressures.

That year our family won the parliamentary elections.

That year – and more particularly in the following year – I began to define myself as a Marxist, and together with friends of mine started to have contacts with members of the party in Beirut and to receive the party's publications regularly.

On the first day of my second year at university, my father was killed. The news reached me while I was in the cinema, watching *Doctor Zhivago* – not because I was keen on the film, but in order to discuss it with my comrades in the party cell, and to study the mechanics of imperialist intrigue against the first socialist revolution in history. *I don't say this sarcastically, Mr Kawabata; please take every letter of what I say seriously.* I was there for the three o'clock showing of the film.

The friend who'd come to give me the news waited for the lights to go up in the cinema during the interval. He was from our village and shared a room with me in lodgings. He came up to the row of seats where I was sitting and beckoned to me to get up and go over to him. After he'd given me the news, I asked him to wait for me in the lodging house until the film had ended. Then I went back to my seat, putting an end to his hopes of persuading me to leave with him immediately.

We reached our village at night.

Darkness falls early in our country, Mr Kawabata, on the first Monday in November – the day the academic year begins in the Lebanese University.

I asked the driver to put me down a few dozen yards from the house, our house, where my father was laid out on a bed borrowed from the neighbours.

When the neighbours saw me getting out of the taxi, they rushed towards me. When they saw me standing and staring silently, they stood silently like me. I could hear the voices of the women wailing and I could see the light of the single lamp in the one-roomed house, spilling out palely through the open door and window. I remember...

I remember well, Mr Kawabata, the darkness that filled the place. Our village had not known public lighting since the French had left the country.

When the neighbours asked me, after a period of silence, whether I wanted to see the body, I said no! Then they led me off to the men's wake in my uncle's house nearby, where, as the deceased's eldest son, I was sat down in the middle of the house beside my brothers, uncles and other relatives.

When the head of the family, our deputy in parliament, arrived, he offered me his condolences, then offered condolences to my brothers and uncles before sitting down immediately beside me, so that anyone else coming in to offer their condolences would have to begin with him first, before moving on to me. His face reeked of perfume as he sat in silence with a distant air, not moving his lips even to return a greeting.

I was aware that he knew of my strange, heretical ideas that were foreign to our country and its traditions, and was aware that he followed my fortunes. In fact, he used to ask my father about me constantly. My father understood what lay behind his questions but could tell him nothing that would give him any pleasure, so he avoided conversation. I was told once that my father had asked him for his advice one day on how to act to keep me under control, but instead of replying he shook his head and kept silent.

I went once with some other people to cry over the corpse, but I couldn't. I couldn't manage a single tear. I believe I simply didn't feel the need for it. Certainly not, in fact!

I stood by the corpse, after the women had made way for us, while my brothers and uncles threw themselves on the murdered man, weeping and wailing over him and swearing to take revenge for their dear one. As I stood like that looking at the body, with the sons and brothers throwing themselves over it, and the women weeping and wailing as they danced around, I remembered one of my French professors in the university. I imagined how he would have collapsed with laughter if he had been present at this scene. The previous year, a young man had died whose family lived in a building next to our college building. His friends had started to dance around with his coffin on the road before the corpse was carried away, and students came out from all the lecture halls to peer down from the windows and balconies. Our class also went out, our French professor with us. When he saw what was happening he burst into hysterical laughter and lost control of himself completely. He was still roaring with laughter even after he had returned to the dais and the students had gone back to their seats. Finally, he managed to get a grip on himself and to say, by way of apology, that this custom was still current to the present day in some places in the French countryside.

After that, I went out before the women could tell the men who were throwing themselves on the body to get up and go away. My action caused astonishment and news of it soon spread. Most people explained it as being the sort of self-control adopted by a man who has suffered a family wound, to stop himself shedding tears before taking revenge and wiping out blood with blood.

After the funeral procession, our deputy had a private conversation with my uncles for some minutes without me, then offered us all his condolences again and left.

At the end of the third day for receiving condolences, my uncles asked me to return to Beirut to continue my studies and complete them without wasting any time. Thanks to the help of our deputy, I would then be able to get a position at a suitable level for the certificate I would be taking, and in this way would be able to support my mother and brothers (my father had left us without any income). They told me I shouldn't be worried on this account at present, as they would share with us every last scrap of bread, and our deputy would never forget us. Before he left on the day of the funeral he had deposited a thousand lira with my mother, part of it donated by him personally and the rest by the family. They also asked me not to return to the village except in case of necessity, since my presence there would be a source of constant anxiety to them, because as I didn't carry weapons and wasn't as careful as I should be, I would be easy prey. When I suggested to them that it might be better to content ourselves with bringing a court case against the murderers and pursuing this rather than trying to hunt one of them down, they said no, we'll open proceedings against them in the same way as they did against us; we won't be satisfied with a court case any more than they were. They then reminded me that we were also from this village, indeed we were its oldest family, in case I'd forgotten, so a court case would neither restore our honour to us, nor restore our standing in the eyes of the other families. In any case, a prison door didn't close on anyone for ever, while the lid of the tomb had shut for ever on your father.

*My father had never gone to prison, because the influence of the head of our family had been strong enough to save him even from litigation.*

Mr Kawabata,

For the whole of this difficult period that we were passing through, my mother didn't say a single word!

She kept her black clothes, and she kept her silence.

Mr Kawabata,

To whom should I reveal what I am going to speak of in the next few moments, if not to you?

At the time of my father's death, my mother was forty years old. She was beautiful, and still in good health, despite having borne ten children, of whom nine survived.

She felt anger and humiliation, I could see that in her eyes. The anger came from what had been hurled at her, by fate, shall we say, rather than by my father. *Unlike me, she certainly didn't make any connection between my father's murder and myself.* The humiliation was because supporting all these souls was far from easy on the basis of the paltry and irregular assistance that my uncles and our deputy were giving her.

I can tell you, Mr Kawabata, that I felt a certain relief

when I noticed that there were several dozen grey hairs (the sign of old age) on my mother's head, and I saw the colour of her hair losing its sheen. *Among us, grey hairs are attributed to anxiety, and anxiety implies the death of the desire for new adventures.* Didn't I tell you, Mr Kawabata, that there are no spontaneous feelings there, but that every feeling lurks ready to spring from the depths of a man's heart? I could add that every sort of future is lurking in the present, that the present is not a walnut tree that bears fruit at the end of the summer, that it is nothing else, that it is not . . . not what?

What is the future, Mr Kawabata? Where does it come from?

From which direction does the future come to us, Mr Kawabata, and how?

For a long time I thought of leaving university to start work, but I couldn't imagine myself away from the university and books, outside the political-intellectual struggle, the struggle for political rights, and even the military–intellectual struggle, if it came to that. We'd discussed the matter several times among ourselves as a group of friends, and I'd discussed it several times with *him*, my friend and comrade whom I'd met in Hamra Street. The view was always that I should continue my studies, because the interests of the party also required it. On one occasion, our meeting was attended by an important party official, who took me to one side after the meeting and told me that I should continue my studies, and that the party would not let me be defeated by material difficulties. He also informed me that it had been decided to give me a considerable sum as a monthly allowance, so that I would be able to get through this difficult period. He told me that my friends and I in the village were rendering the party services of incalculable value, and that the party was in great need of bases among the Christian section of the population generally, and the Maronites in particular – especially as our party was the only one of all the leftist and Palestinian groups able to work within this community and to attract groups of people within it. This would consolidate our position with the Palestinian resistance, who still refused to acknowledge our importance on the Lebanese stage.

I refused to take a single lira from the party, Mr Kawabata, I can confirm that to you. He – my friend and comrade – reproached me on several occasions, because his analysis took as its starting-point his constant slogan: Everything for the sake of the party! My own opinion was that, precisely for the sake of carrying out this slogan to the letter, we should refuse to take any remuneration for our work for the struggle, especially if this work was directly connected with the party.

*You will doubtless detect in what I say a desire on my part to demonstrate the purity of my inner self and the sincerity of my commitment. Yes! I sometimes surprise myself thinking that you are a perfect woman. A princess, a virgin, desiring but hesitant. And I strive, that her choice may fall on me.*

At that time, little more than a year had passed since I had made his acquaintance, but our friendship had become deep and firm. Scarcely a day went by without my meeting him.

Mr Kawabata,

The first time I went to Hamra Street it was in his company. *He had come to Beirut two years before me.* That area was just beginning to flourish. He pointed out to me people whose names we were reading in the papers, not just Lebanese but other Arabs too – refugees from unstable, reactionary, *petit-bourgeois* regimes, that feared the fundamental revolutionary change for which the working class was struggling, together with their revolutionary intellectual allies, who believed in the idea of the working class and its historical role.

'If this Lebanon whose regime we're trying to change is a safe refuge for them,' I said to him once, 'how much worse must their own regimes be!' 'Don't be deceived for a moment by the formal freedom to be found in Lebanon,' he replied. 'In the first place, it is imposed on the regime by the daily struggle that the working class is engaged in, and secondly it is no more than a façade. True freedom means mankind freeing itself from class exploitation.' I shared his view, but I also said to him: 'Isn't it a strange paradox that the regimes that expelled them and expelled the Palestinian guerrillas – as we used to call them – should be our allies and the allies of the Palestinian resistance against the Lebanese regime?' He replied that the class struggle was an extremely complicated matter, and that our alliance with these regimes was only temporary, since our victory in Lebanon would have dire results for them. Then he sighed and said: 'They – the regimes, that is – are like a man licking his own wounds.'

Comrade Hasan was with us constantly My other friend was secretary of the branch at that time, and their links were old and well established. They had both gone to university two years before me, and they had both been in the party before university.

The three of us trained together in the use of weapons, combat methods and the principles of popular wars of liberation (our model was Vietnam) in a camp belonging to a Palestinian organization that was intellectually close to the party. We learned how to eat snakes if we were forced to, after ripping their heads from their bodies, and we underwent a baptism of fire by crossing through blazing barricades while bullets were fired at us. We took Kalashnikovs to pieces and reassembled them at night in total darkness, climbed over electric fences and, bristling with arms, crossed water channels, suspended from ropes above them or sunk in them up to our necks. We learned to contain sudden enemy attacks, then returned them.

We were trained in reaching confiscated territory and in dealing with the methods of the treacherous Israelis. We showed our Palestinian comrades the extent of our seriousness of commitment, as a party, to the cause. We got to know them at close quarters. We liked them and they liked us, and they especially liked my friend, as he'd given a number of lectures about the organic connection between the Palestinian cause – the Arabs' first cause – and the cause of the working class within the Lebanese state.

This period of training – the first I had experienced – lasted for three weeks. My mother had no news of me for that period (she knew nothing about the matter at all) and I likewise had no news of her. One evening towards the end of the second week, while we were resting after supper, I felt a longing for her. I told him about it (communication with the outside world was forbidden) and he smiled, making no comment. Despite the embarrassment that I felt at this mingling of childish emotions with the serious work of the struggle, I asked him why he had smiled. He answered that we needed time for the cause we were struggling for to become the mother we longed for.

*Mr Kawabata, these were his exact words after receiving an*

*inaccurate report of his mother's death by random sniper fire
that hit her house (this was at the beginning of the civil war in
Lebanon): 'I will marry, to have a daughter who will be mine
alone for ever, for I will have a greater claim to her than any
other man.' He surprised me by this reaction, the meaning and
necessity for which I did not understand. He shocked me so
much that, despite the delicacy of the moment, I could not
restrain myself from asking him angrily: 'Will you have
children by her?' He looked at me angrily with a look that I
had never seen before and was about to speak, but he thought
better of it.*

*'So far as I am concerned,' said Hasan, by way of comment
on his remark, 'I shall not marry, so as not to have children.'*

*Mr Kawabata,*

*I have still not understood the meaning of his reaction to the
news of his mother's death. But I well remember that he later
began bitterly to criticize the prevailing morality among us, and
to call in his meetings for women to be public property.*

*Once, during the same period, I told him of my admiration
for a woman who was close to us politically. He immediately
told me with a smile how only a week ago, after he had
ejaculated inside her and got up off her, she in turn had got up
and he'd started to urinate over her, while she twisted and
turned this way and that, so that his puddle of water could
reach the whole of her body.*

*'Why do you tell it in such a sarcastic, humiliating way?' I
said. 'Doesn't everyone have the right to take his most intimate
pleasure as he wishes?'*

*And he smiled.*

Mr Kawabata,

When he made fun of me for missing my mother, I
felt no disgust for him, or even anger. On the contrary,
I appreciated his forward–looking viewpoint, and his

total immersion in the cause. I said to myself: 'I still have a lot to do!'

When he made that astonishing statement after being told of his mother's death, my angry reaction was not caused by disgust, but from a feeling that I'd lost my footing, so to speak. What he'd said didn't belong to our intellectual world at all. This gave me a dreadful sensation of alienation and lack of direction – like a sleeper who opens his eyes during the night, and finds himself nowhere, directionless, in a void.

*Mr Kawabata,*

*I must tell you here that by this time he had started to criticize some of the actions of the party, and even some elements of its political line, while for my part I held so closely to the party that my friends were beginning to describe me as a fanatic.*


Mr Kawabata,

Hatred is something I came to know, but later – twelve years after that, in fact, on the day that I met him on Hamra Street and for a moment thought that I was seeing myself. This wasn't the first time I'd met him since we'd left the party and each of us gone his own way, but it was the first time that my whole being had been shaken. *Mr Kawabata, I don't exactly know what it means for a being to be shaken, but I can tell you that I am unable to resist expressions of this sort that steal through me and permeate my letter to you.*

There was not a fold or a wrinkle on his face or neck!

Smooth-faced as a child, with a neck that filled the collar of his shirt, without bursting out of it.

A face brimming with purity; a virginal smile. A neck free from the trace of even a spot of blood, even the spot of blood that oozes from a cut made by a razor blade. The

108

face of a man who sleeps as soon as his head hits the pillow, with an easy conscience, pure white like snow.

In the past I'd met him every so often, but hadn't used to greet him, and he hadn't greeted me. Like two strangers. I'd never met him except on Hamra Street, his refuge and the only place where he didn't feel lonely, the only place where he wasn't afraid he would die. The sniping might be like rain in winter, but he would stay put until the assistants shut the café doors, when he would leave with the last one and stand uncertainly on the pavement for some time, thinking where to go to spend the remaining daylight, until evening came and he could gamble until dawn.

In the past, however, he hadn't worn the smart outfit he was wearing now. His style of dress had been more in tune with his social status and hadn't attracted attention, either positive or negative.

What had happened, then, for him to go up in the world like this? Where had he acquired this sense of superiority he relied on to walk with his head inclined a little backwards, staring ahead so that passers-by got out of his way, while for his part he didn't need to avoid anyone?

What did he see now in the distance, when almost everyone was agreed that the war had probably ended, and that the period of peace hoped for for more than a lifetime had probably begun? *Was it true that everyone was hoping for peace though peace didn't come? Why not?*

Was he trying to catch a glimpse of the peace that was coming?

Then again, I saw him smiling ever so faintly, looking into the distance over other people's heads, as if he were afraid that the camera of history might surprise him while he was in a non-historical position.

Smiling!

How this smile annoyed me!

If we approach nature, Mr Kawabata, from a standpoint of equality, it will be unjust! This is something I have accepted and always tried to adapt to. But when to the injustice of nature is added the injustice of man, then life is impossible!

He was several years older than me. I was still not yet twenty-two when my hair began to fall out and it was only a few months since I had become acquainted with him.

I wasn't conscious of old age on that day but of injustice!

It was injustice that scared me then, rather than the feeling that life had begun to slip away, because life for me during that period was opening doors on the future. *Notice this expression, Mr Kawabata: 'opening doors on'. I shall not call your attention to these eternally beautiful expressions each time they steal into the fabric of my letter to you, so as not to disrupt the flow of your reading.* The future was still distant and beautiful and certain. *Was it really pressing? What exactly was it?*

When I told him, with some hesitation, that I'd consulted a doctor and that he'd prescribed injections for me to stimulate the hair follicles, he laughed until he almost choked (*that's how we sometimes describe someone who is roaring with laughter*).

The fact is, Mr Kawabata, that I had hesitated for a long time before going to a doctor, probably for the same reasons that made him laugh.

His view of the matter, in a nutshell, was that we still needed a long time to be able to settle our accounts with our *petit-bourgeois* conscience. He used the plural when he said it, because the individual was something not worth mentioning, merely a network of social relationships.

By this time we had read the philosophical works of Marx and Engels, as well as the *Communist Manifesto*, and discussed them at length.

I remember that I hesitated for a long time before telling him about my visit to the doctor. In fact, I also hesitated for a long time before I decided to go.

And for the same reasons!

Or perhaps because a bald head is a disgrace, and going to the doctor is a clear admission of it.

His view, therefore, was that in terms of our revolutionary commitment we (we intellectuals, that is) hadn't yet reached the stage of total immersion in the cause of the working class, and that we hadn't yet assimilated ourselves to the cause sufficiently for it to become a spontaneous feeling on our part.

A *petit-bourgeois* intellectual of country origins, with a father who earned his living from (private) land-ownership and work as a craftsman, could not assimilate himself to the cause of the working class overnight. For the revolutionary intellectual, unlike the worker, revolutionary reactions had to be acquired. This demanded much effort, self-control, caution and reflection, though it was certainly possible.

Was Lenin a worker?

The face of a man who sleeps as soon as his head hits the pillow, Mr Kawabata, and who enjoys a clear conscience.

I well remember.

I who remember well.

It was twenty-two years ago, in 1969, in the cafeteria of the College of Education in the Lebanese University. We were putting the finishing touches to our plan to take part in the demonstration, the famous demon-stration of 23 April.

He was nervous and agitated, coming and going for no reason.

I remember.

One of our comrades called him the 'mother of the bridegroom' that day. *It's a metaphor used among us for a person who is in a hurry and preoccupied with a thousand things at the same time.*

The demonstration was his day. *Among us Arabs, the word 'day' is also used to mean a 'battle', and 'days' to mean 'battledays'. The Arabs used the term 'battledays' with no mention of nights, because their wars were fought by day; when their battles were fought at night, they mentioned the fact specifically.* He prepared the slogans, fixed the place for us to meet at the start of the demonstration, reviewed all possible contingencies and prescribed a solution for each of them. He was certain that the security forces would open fire on the demonstrators, and this increased his agitation.

He thought that the success of this demonstration would increase the appeal of Palestinian guerrilla action launched from Lebanese soil.

Indeed, he went even further in his imagination. He thought that the demonstration would lead to the start of the process (he said it in French, *processus*) of bringing down the Lebanese regime, and then the other Arab regimes, which would lead to the assumption of power by the working-class parties and their allies. Then the popular war of liberation against Israel would begin in earnest.

He was not a Maoist, but he liked to repeat the famous saying of Mao Tse-tung: 'Imperialism is a paper tiger' on every possible occasion. 'How about its offspring, then?' he used to add.

He was almost killed that day.

I was carrying him on my shoulder as he shouted the slogans we'd prepared in advance. Sometimes he improvised, and we repeated them afterwards.

When the bullets were fired we didn't hear them. At first we just saw people running away. Then we ran away ourselves and were dispersed.

We were dispersed! *Meaning that, after being a group, we were split up.*

He himself had seen what was happening from the first minute, as he was being carried on my shoulders.

I didn't understand what he meant when he began to get agitated. He didn't say to me explicitly that he wanted to get down, but I helped him down mechanically without being conscious of anything in particular.

'They're firing tear gas,' he said, as he ran towards the entrance of an old building. I ran behind him. My eyes had begun to hurt as they became flooded with tears and I had difficulty breathing. When I reached the entrance I saw him collapsed on the staircase opposite a policeman, who was pulling at the gun strapped to his shoulder against his body.

Unlike him, I didn't collapse on to the staircase, for my strength had not entirely failed me.

The policeman opened his eyes. They bulged so much that I thought they would spill out of their sockets. He looked at my friend with these eyes, and my friend looked back. Their eyes met. Then they closed them, so that each could go away to attend to his own pain – or so I imagined, because some moments later I saw him get up and throw himself on the policeman with an animal movement, with all the determination (or what was left of it) he possessed, trying to snatch the gun that the policeman was unconsciously gripping instinctively, without getting up. When he repeated the attempt, the policeman shook, but still didn't get up, so he went back and lay down again. I hurried over and helped him get up, afraid that the policeman might recover his strength and arrest him.

The policeman stared at him as we were going out and spat, but his saliva got no further than his lips and ran down his chin.

When I told him the story later, he told me off and said that I should have told him at the time, so that he could have gone back to him and kicked him in the mouth with his foot. To make him spit blood. The agent, the dog, the instrument of state oppression. We exposed ourselves to all sorts of dangers for his sake and the sake of his children. *One of his slogans in demonstrations went as follows: 'Policeman, your son's a student; throw away your weapon and join us.'*

Bullets were still being fired and the square was beginning to empty of demonstrators, who had been dispersed in every direction. I was looking around hoping to find my friends, but they had split up. He and I made for a back street where we were lucky enough to find a taxi which took us – as we had agreed – downtown, that is to the Burj, or Martyrs' Square.

Martyrs' Square!
Martyrs' Square!


Dear Mr Kawabata,

You will not deprive me now of the pleasure of talking about Martyrs' Square! You will see how much this will interest you.

However much the Sunni Muslims who live there say that it is an artificial creation, separated by (French) imperialism from the main body of the Arab nation as they divided it up into separate units – and however much the Christians deny it and say that it is a country with roots stretching back to the dawn of history – Lebanon today is an independent state, a member of the United Nations and the Arab League, with a capital, the city of Beirut, in the middle of the country on the Mediterranean coast.

Lebanon has a capital, just as every other state has a capital.

And just as every other state has a main square – one at least – which is usually given a name carrying some national significance, so it is with us.

Exactly.

*Before I continue to pour out my soul, let me confide in you that Lebanon is one of those countries that produces nothing but its own periodic tragedies.*

*Countries like the grass on mud roofs, beautiful, growing quickly only to catch fire with the first warmth of the sun.*

*Mr Kawabata,*

*Lebanon,*

*Lebanon was a country far too beautiful for the region to be able to extinguish her desires.*

*Trop beau!*

We called our capital's main square Martyrs' Square by official decree, but it was popularly known as 'Downtown' or 'Burj Square'. Before the war it was the heart of the capital, with its markets, banks, cinemas, popular theatres, hotels and red-light district, and its bus stations and taxi ranks served by vehicles from every part of Lebanon. It was the heart of Lebanon.

Today, this square and the area around it have been destroyed almost completely as a result of the war, because for seventeen years it was the dividing line between the warring factions, between the two Beiruts: East Beirut and West Beirut.

I wish I could speak to you at greater length about this square and the area around it, but I find myself extremely upset. Nor is this the first time that I find myself upset from speaking about this square.

I have often tried and not been able to. I have often been asked and not been able to. And I always wonder about the reason!

*You will note: I am always looking for the reason!*

*Love me, Mr Kawabata. Take me as I am, with all my contradictions, for it is beyond the power of my brain not to pursue the reason, and it is beyond my capacity not to see a reason for everything!*

*History, Mr Kawabata, is a poisonous being! It makes us think that it is running when in fact it just goes on.*

*Water runs, the wind runs, the sun runs, horses run.*

*Custom runs, we run on a path.*

*The slave girl was called* jariya *('runner') because she was made to run in service, to run for her living, in fact. As if there were nothing that did not run, when in fact everything just goes on.*

*Or contracts or disappears.*

*We are not alone then in letting words run away with us wherever they will, or in running away with them wherever we will, while he, the poisonous being − history − just goes on.*

*Mr Kawabata, I hate history as I hate death, and meaninglessness.*

*An emptiness dissolving into space.*

*A tyrant. And a beast.*

*History is a beast. But not like a mountain. With bitterness, rather.*

I was driven to make these observations by my telling you that I am always wondering about the reason but, whether or not there is a reason, I still feel extremely upset when Martyrs' Square is being talked about.

I don't like it when a man tries to achieve greatness for himself too easily.

Film-makers have taken shots there, photographers have taken pictures there, and journalists written articles about the place. Visitors pay visits, tourists travel there and there is now an improvised café at the feet of the statue of the martyrs in the middle of the square.

Concerts, song recitals and sound-and-light shows have been held there, in some of which children have taken part – children, of course, being a token of peace and the future. *This, despite the fact that a certain modesty and sense of propriety are more usual among us Arabs.* Reports of these events stirred in me a desire to disappear, I mean to melt away into nothingness, to become a thing forgotten.

But before I let my words run away with me, I shall stop them, I shall stop speaking to ask myself: 'Is this really what is upsetting me?'

I doubt that.

What I am certain about is that *something* is upsetting me. *It is not easy to explain.*

I will try to tackle the subject from another angle. A French friend said to me after visiting the commercial centre:

*C'est beau!*

*C'est poétique!*

Beautiful, pure poetry!

I raised my voice in her face to protest that this was my country, destroyed by evil hands – you will doubtless have noticed the rhetorical tone, Mr Kawabata – and, as if she had expected this reaction on my part, she apologized immediately, even before I had finished speaking, and urged me not to continue. I remained silent, as if under protest – I mean, it looked as if I was remaining silent under protest, but I was not. I continued my angry words, but in my heart. 'You are people in need of something to shake your feelings,' I said to her, 'because you have no problems. You have got everything and everyone that you desired, and have lost the power to feel.'

*Exotica!*

She heard me mutter this word and looked as though she would like the earth to swallow her up, she was so embarrassed. Exactly as I would now like the earth to swallow me up, Mr Kawabata, as I write these words.

*C'est beau!*

*C'est poétique!*

These words expressed exactly how I felt also!

In fact, I wasn't actually upset by my friend, but by a disturbing feeling that could not be overcome by the poetic nature of the dreadful destruction. The feeling of embarrassment was made worse by the painful memories of the suffering we had experienced, the humiliation we had endured, and the fear we had felt. There, and in every place like it.

As I pen these words, Mr Kawabata, I ask myself: 'Why be embarrassed at those feelings?'

Why the embarrassment, especially as I am always trying to hold to the following principle: 'Do not be embarrassed at anything you feel, for all kinds of feelings are always lurking in the depths of a man's heart, but keep the bad feelings suppressed!' *Ah! this deep pit that it is impossible to get out of!*

I am not one of those people, Mr Kawabata, who believe in the sanctity of place, not one of those who believe that there is a conspiracy on the part of history in the architecture of a place. I am rather inclined to the belief that between the architecture of a place and the events that take place in it, there is a link, but only *a posteriori*. It is not because of the nature of a place that particular events happen there. It is not because of the nature of the Rawsha rocks off the coast of Beirut that people commit suicide from the top of them. Any high place is suitable for suicide – balconies, roofs, cliffs, etc., etc.

*I confess that the rocks of Rawsha are tempting.*

I spent four whole years in that room overlooking Martyrs' Square. I was a student. A large room with four beds in it. Three of them were for me and two fellow-students, the fourth was for passing customers. This bed was our constant nightmare, for we didn't know who we would have to put up with: smelly feet and snoring we especially abhorred. He would always go to bed before us and we would be forced to go out. He divided us.

The three of us in the room had a single set of political convictions. We used to pay the price of the extra bed so as to keep it for ourselves twice a week at least, and usually my friend or Hasan would sleep there. Otherwise, we would invite some other friends of ours, and talk about the subjects that concerned us as party members and revolutionary intellectuals, until late at night.

I remember...

About a month after my arrival at the hotel, I went out on to the balcony to look at the military parade celebrating Independence Day. That day was a shock. The soldiers weren't like those in the book we had studied at school, they were all colliding with each other. Those in the rear would push those in front, then those in front would turn round to return the compliment. I decided that they were traitors. Or that they didn't love their country. This was the first time I had seen a military parade.

I remember...

I was always going out on to the balcony to watch a traffic policeman who was stationed in the square. He was clever. I used to watch the cars passing under the balcony, and especially I used to stare at the feet and legs of the women.

I remember...

In the square there were glass booths. Public telephones. I had nobody to telephone from them, but I very much liked seeing them. Something about them attracted me, perhaps the fact that they were deserted, night and day. Glass. In a public square.

A man went into one of them once to telephone and I stood watching him. After a few moments I saw him hitting the receiver so hard that he broke it. I ran towards him but he gestured to me to go away, so I ran to a policeman some way off, but he paid me no attention. I would have liked to have told this policeman that the man in the telephone box was a relative of the undisciplined soldiers on parade, or at least from the same village. I was sure he was.

One year, a flower clock was constructed in the middle of the square. Its hands moved over a circular bed of flowers, and the figures were also made of flowers.

I used to love (and still do love) public places.

When he described these feelings of mine as *petit-bourgeois*, I kept silent. 'They want to prettify their ugliness for us!' he used to like to say. 'Everything they do, in the final analysis, is simply to tighten their grip on the working class.'

He was like a mountain, Mr Kawabata, like a mountain.

Mountains in our tradition, Kawabata, are mighty and

majestic. They are used as a metaphor for firmness, solidity and pride.

When I told him what had happened to me after an argument at college about the existence of God, he smiled. I told him that I'd had stomach contractions and almost spewed my guts on to the pavement. I would have done, had it not been for a last vestige of strength that allowed me to reach a café toilet. I was in the College of Education at the Lebanese University at the time. The discussion was about the existence of God, and the arguments against his existence were more substantial than those for it.

At that time 'against' represented the future, and 'for' was the past. In one camp there was the liberation of Palestine; socialism; the alliance with the Soviet Union, Third World liberation movements, and progressive forces in the capitalist states, and the non-existence of God – while in the opposite camp were ranged objectively Israel; imperialism; the Arab regimes, and God.

During that discussion I felt that God had deserted me, for he had disappeared, and I felt a searing pain in every part of me, in the whole of my being. I left the session while it was still going on, and got into a service taxi that was going I didn't know where. A few moments after getting into the taxi I vomited violently, so hard that there was nothing left in my stomach. This made the driver angry. 'You might have done it before!' he said, and I felt sorry.

I felt sorry to the depths of my being. I wish I'd been able to say to him that all this pain that I was suffering was for his sake, that vomiting up the contents of my stomach was simply a *rite de passage* from one camp to the other, and that I was now in his camp, with an objective interest in the disappearance of God, and consequently of religion – the opium and anaesthetic of the people, and the ally of the ruling class.

He smiled when I told him that. The mountain smiled. *It wasn't the difference in height that jolted my being when I met him and he didn't see me. The man never saw anything unless he chose to see it, especially when it was I who'd wanted it that way. No, it was something else, Kawabata, something else.* By way of general observation, he said that we still had a long way to go to free ourselves from our heritage and become revolutionaries in every sense of the word. This was a difficult thing, requiring a daily struggle against the self on all fronts, especially on the fronts that appeared unimportant – like our everyday language, for example, which was full of expressions with the word God in them: God willing, Praise be to God, by God's leave, etc. These expressions were symptoms of deep-seated, unconscious convictions implying submission to fate and a lack of trust in the human will. This was exactly what the ruling class wanted to establish to perpetuate their rule.

Like a mountain, Kawabata, like a mountain.

He became even more stubborn after his return from France where he'd spent several years completing a doctorate on political science, while I finished a doctorate in literature. The most important thing for us, however, was not the degree, but the rich experience of the struggle alongside our comrades in the French Communist Party, which we joined for the period of our stay there. We participated in educational and training programmes, took part in the struggles in which the party was engaged, and communicated the rightness of the Palestinian cause to as many circles as we were able, in cooperation with the progressive Arab organizations (Palestinian ones in particular) who were represented there.

We returned from France proud of our experience and determined to use it in the service of the party and the cause of the working class.

We returned with greater faith in our principles and convictions, greater even than our French comrades themselves. He once said to one of our French comrades after she'd informed us that she was soon to marry: 'Do people still marry at the end of the twentieth century?'

To emphasize the cutting of the umbilical cord with the childish longing for the countryside, after our return I decided never to feel nostalgia for my mother's olives, her olive oil, or for anything made with her own hands.

*He hated olive trees. His father had died while working among them. He was picking olives in autumn, just before noon in the heat of the sun, when a snake started up and bit him, and he died.*

I also decided that in cheap, popular restaurants I would eat the things that my mother made at home herself. 'The whole city must turn into a mother's embrace.' This was my slogan, which overwhelmed me with happiness when I was able to formulate it in this way. I was also very pleased that *he* liked it.

Everything we ate in restaurants must be the same sort as our mothers made at home in the village.

Beirut had not yet changed into a mother's embrace when I started eating in cheap restaurants there. Daily bread among the masses. Like the masses.

I used to choose types of food that I'd particularly enjoyed eating at my mother's house. They tasted different, but it was only a phase, and afterwards all sorts of food tasted good again.

One day after supper in a restaurant, he took me to hospital in his car. When I was returning the following day, he said that what had happened to me the day before might happen to anyone anywhere! I agreed with him before he had finished speaking, for I had been thinking of the thing in the same way.

Beirut must turn into a city of individuals, free from the ties of family, countryside, sect and tribal affiliation.

This was what a city was!

Beirut must become like the cities described in the books we used to read, so that our principles could become effective there. We had fashioned our ideas; all we had to do now was to fashion Beirut in accordance with those ideas.

So...

He contacted his girlfriend's father by telephone and told him – I was standing beside him, giving him advice with whispers and gestures: 'Your daughter has now come of age, she is free to do and say what she likes.' Then he made an appointment with him. I went with him to the appointment.

It was early evening, at the beginning of the Lebanese war in 1975.

We arrived before him at the restaurant where we'd agreed to meet. Luckily, however, we hadn't gone inside but were waiting for him on the pavement.

I remember that I was nervous in the meantime. I told him I was nervous and suggested frankly that our position possibly depended on an analysis lacking in some basic data. I also told him that our behaviour was perhaps somewhat idealistic, but I quickly corrected myself and told him that we had to confront reality in order to shake it, otherwise everything would remain as it was for ever.

When her father arrived, he got out of the car evidently nervous and immediately went towards the car boot. I hurried after him to see what he was doing, guessing that he was intending to take out a weapon. When I saw him actually take out a revolver, I grabbed him. I shouted to my friend and he came up, but instead of helping me to disarm him, he started reprehending him. *His girlfriend had told him that her father was a Marxist, in other words that he didn't mind if his daughter married a Christian.*

So he started to make a speech: 'We are at the start of the twenty-first century (only a quarter of a century away). This behaviour is unacceptable today.'

The father, however, was becoming more agitated and nervous – so agitated, in fact, that I had not a shred of doubt that if I left him with the revolver, he would fire into both our stomachs.

His revolver had become our only hope. The man, however, was able to reach the trigger with his finger and pull it, firing the first shot into the air, then a second, also into the air, then a third into my friend's thigh. The blood flowed. He then let go of the revolver, which I was still holding on to, went back to his car and drove off.

My friend shouted to me not to fire on him. I had already taken aim and was ready to fire.

My friend's wound was, fortunately for him (and for me, of course), quite superficial.

'To the hospital!' I said.

'No,' he said, 'let's go back home.'

So we went back home, where he proceeded to treat himself. When I suggested to him that we send for a friend of ours who was a doctor, he refused, but I summoned him anyway.

During the days that followed, people began to mediate – friends and acquaintances, that is. A 'truce' was concluded, when the father visited his stubborn 'son-in-law'.

'See?' he said to me, after the father had left.

My friend meant that he had been right. I reminded him that I had never opposed his initiative. On the contrary, I had been one of its supporters. He reminded me of my unease, and I reminded him of his unease, and especially of his silence.

This incident also increased his confidence in the strength and efficacy of his ideas. 'The individual – male or female' (he didn't like using the word 'man') – 'is free to say and do what he or she likes.' This was a general principle that could be applied wherever one was.

I can tell you now, however, Mr Kawabata – you, and you alone – that although I was pleased at the visit of his girlfriend's father at the time, in a part of myself I was also deeply suspicious. Why had the father changed his mind so quickly and easily? Had he become a secularist accepting mixed marriages between different religious communities, at a time when we instinctively felt that the world was entering on a long winter of bloodshed between all the different parties, but particularly between the various religious communities? This winter had in fact already started, though we, progressive combatants, refused to see things in reality that contradicted our beliefs. That was too much for us – despite the fact that from the first few weeks of the war the party had been distributing to us Christian members (including the combatants among us) identity cards belonging to the armed Palestinian organizations who effectively controlled the territory, along with borrowed Muslim names. On my identity card my name was Muhammad Ayyub, born in Jaffa (Palestine), and my profession was given as 'combatant'.

We didn't see any particular danger in this. We didn't ask or wonder how it was that we had to be Muslims so as not to be a target for abduction or murder in the areas we were defending with arms. How, then, could we criticize the Phalange for their sectarian operations?

We didn't see any particular danger in this. Rather, we saw in it a striking concern on the part of the party for its supporters, at a time when it was being plunged into a bitter struggle on several fronts.

Then the father disappeared from our sights, and stopped bothering us. His girlfriend began to visit him with greater freedom. Her father continued to insist, not on marriage, but at least that it shouldn't go on too long.

It had, frankly, become difficult for the father to stand as an obstacle in the way of his daughter's wish to marry my friend, after he'd got to know him and after his fellow-comrades had spoken to him about him at length. He wasn't just anyone, he was one of the party's leading intellectuals, one of its most valiant fighters. He was the hero of 23 April 1969.

The day he really came into his own, his day! The day the state security forces tried to take over Martyrs' Square.

The time was early evening, and we were putting into effect the plan we had drawn up earlier, forming small, mobile groups, so that as soon as one group was put out of action or dispersed, another group would form, announcing itself with slogans directed against the repressive regime.

My friend was everywhere. Shots were fired in his direction several times and he was almost hit. Each time he escaped he became more agitated.

I was constantly by his side, whichever way he was

heading. He once asked me to withdraw and to abandon a position because the situation, he said, was changing for the worse and becoming extremely dangerous. I immediately answered that we should therefore all withdraw. I would also have liked to have said to him that courage did not consist in exposing oneself as an easy target when there wasn't any need for it.

I too was almost hit. *I didn't tell him that.* A bullet almost grazed my ear, but I didn't tell anyone that. *How, then, could I see him exposing himself to danger when he didn't see me? And why?* Because the struggle in my eyes meant silent self-sacrifice. And because training the spotlight on an individual, on a heroic leader, was the sort of reactionary exercise that we had to escape from. The masses were the true heroes, the stars, and it was on them that all the spotlights should be trained. This was a pure revolutionary exercise. The other way was a bourgeois operation that would lead us to the deification of the individual, and give him a role in history that didn't belong to him.

It was the masses that made history, not the leader. Every deification of the individual was a negation of the role of the masses. It was the duty of the masses to acquire the necessary experience and to build it up so as to be able to take history by storm. The more the masses declined to make an assault on history themselves, history would remain as it was, and injustice would remain in existence. There would be no escape for mankind, no promised dawn would break.

This is what I wanted to say to my friend, this is what I wanted to remind him of, rather, in those crazy moments. But he was alone, I mean he was full of his loneliness; I mean, it was impossible for anyone else to reach him, to add anything to him, or take anything from him. He was seeking his own death. Martyrdom. For it is martyrdom alone in decisive moments like this that can bring history to fruition, spurring it on to take the decisive steps towards socialism. Towards freedom, justice and equality.

*He had never before received news like the news of the attempted murder of his girlfriend. After her father had realized that nothing would deflect her from achieving her goal of marrying him, he sent the rest of the family to their village, and connected a gas pipe to reach the room where she was sleeping. He left it on all night, and in the morning carried her lifeless body into the kitchen, turned off the gas and left. But she hadn't died. After that her comrades decided to send her on a scholarship to specialize in medicine in Moscow, because the situation in the country wouldn't allow a front to be opened at the present time with the reactionary Muslims, to the detriment of the basic struggle against the Lebanese regime.*

At that time people hadn't yet got used to seeing martyrs fall every day in their scores and hundreds. The war hadn't yet begun. Six long years still separated us from 1975.

The fall of a martyr in those days was a very serious matter – a matter that shook the country to its core. It could force a government to resign, and the funeral procession would attract front-page headlines in the newspapers.

We used to name our children, our schools, and our institutions after them. When we mentioned them, we would remain silent for a few moments, and if we were sitting would make a point of standing in their honour.

At that time every martyr was a distinguished martyr – not like today, when martyrs come in tens of thousands, but few of them are distinguished.

Mr Kawabata,

Listen to what I wrote when some of us fell as martyrs at the beginning of the war, and we liked to call ourselves the Martyrs' Party. I said:

*Those who repeat that art is the opposite of commitment, seem to those who read the epic of our martyrs like the stumps of rotten teeth.*

*These people are happy when they beat their mothers at a game of cards, while the town squares are open to the winds.*

*These people's stomachs churn at the sight of blood . . .*

Mr Kawabata,

I wrote these words a few weeks after the murder of a comrade by my side, when we were on guard duty one night in a flat at the top of a building whose occupants had fled because it was on the front line. We were alone and if we saw anything suspicious, one of us had to go down to pass on the information, while the other stayed watching. Suddenly we were the target for some bursts of fire which lasted for a good two or three minutes. We immediately threw ourselves to the ground, and started crawling in the direction of the inner rooms that were safer. After the firing had stopped, I felt that I had lost control both of my bodily organs and mental faculties, and of my sensations. My heart was beating on its own with a quite frightening rhythm as if it had no connection with me or the other organs of my body. My hands were shaking and the gun I was holding in them banged against my head. Only one thing would obey me: my voice. After a while, however, when I heard it going its own way with obscure words, and letters and syllables which fell into no logical order, I started to choose the words and utter them one at a time so as to be sure that they were under my control. After I'd pulled myself together, and the parts of my body had regained their cohesion, I heard a faint moaning in the distance and called out. There was no answer, but the moaning continued. That was when I came to realize that my friend had been hit, and that I had to reach him as quickly as possible. But how? I'd lost my sense of direction, and I couldn't use the light from the cigarette lighter. Despite taking all due precautions, we'd lit several cigarettes and this had probably given away our position in the first place. I finally managed to reach him, how I don't know, but when my hand touched him I felt that it had touched a pool of blood. 'Don't be afraid,' I said to him, not yet knowing anything about his injury. 'It's only a superficial wound.' When he heard my voice he said:

'Recite the *fatiha*.'*

At first I thought that I hadn't heard properly. He was speaking in a scarcely audible voice. I asked him why, but he simply repeated, with the last remaining vestige of will-power that was in him:

'Recite the *fatiha*.'

The request stunned me. Deep in my heart I wished that I could recite the *fatiha* for him, but I didn't know it. At the same time, I didn't want to refuse him a request at such a decisive moment as the one he was passing through. So I quickly muttered some phrases that I improvised on the spot, including the name of God, then left him and went to tell our comrades that he'd been injured.

After we'd taken him down, Mr Kawabata, I saw his body in the light of the room where we laid him out. It was bathed in blood. It seems that the first volley had hit him with full force.

---

*Opening chapter of the Qur'an

We couldn't carry his corpse out until the afternoon of the next day. It was hot, summery weather at the time.

The roast flesh of a man, Mr Kawabata, and the roast meat of an animal are so alike that it is hard to tell them apart.

My stomach also used to really churn at the sight of blood. I won't hide from you what I effectively hid from myself – namely, that my problems with eating meat began at the start of the war, and especially with that incident, when I saw human flesh roast in shrapnel.

Many other people besides myself also stopped eating meat. One woman, the day she saw a charred corpse, didn't just stop eating meat, she became unable to sleep except in water. Then, when this proved impossible, she started to urinate in her bed in order to sleep. Another woman collected all the cats of the district together and put contraceptive pills in their food, explaining that she hated to see cats reproduce.

The piece of news that I'm going to convey to you didn't reach you before your death, so let me tell it to you:

When they started to clear away the front lines in Beirut and open up the roads between the two halves of our capital, news got around to the effect that dogs were raiding the city. They'd been forced to flee from the no man's land on either side of the dividing lines, where they'd fed for fifteen years on human corpses that no one had been able to reach to bury, because of the continuous fighting and exchanges of sniper fire. Reports said that these hungry dogs were attacking populated areas at night, preying on humans, especially women and children, and prowling in packs as they used to in times gone by before the planet was civilized. With my own eyes – *I almost said 'with the mother of my eyes', another of our Arabic expressions of eternal beauty* – I saw a bald man with long sideburns and a long beard wandering about, with several centimetres of dirt on his skin and clothes, carrying a crook like a shepherd. He had a pack of dogs around him that looked much the same as he did, and he was running, as if someone from the front line had told him that the situation there had become very dangerous and that he must get there quickly. The pack around him was obviously also eager to get there.

The news of dogs hungry for human flesh excited the imagination of the city, Mr Kawabata. There was a lot of talk about it and there was a lot of killing of dogs.

Another rumour doing the rounds was that, as well as beef, lamb and goat's meat, people throughout the city were eating meat from dogs, either hunted especially for the purpose, or whose corpses were being collected up from here and there in the streets and city centre.

To return to the article that I wrote about the importance of martyrdom, I said then: 'These people's stomachs churn at the sight of blood, and they proclaim their love. But the tons of misery must not be weighed.'

What I meant, Mr Kawabata, was that these people who preach love but whose hearts are nauseated and revolted by killing, these people don't want to see the misery in which the vast majority of mankind live, weighed down by its burden, and don't want to take it into account. *I nearly said 'into the eye of the account'!*

I was with history, then. The revolution was a historical necessity, and what was happening in Lebanon was the beginning of the revolution. Every obstacle in the way of the revolution was an obstacle to the movement of history. *I'd have very much liked to have said 'the march of history'!*

*My love,*

*Should I compare it with the walk of a partridge?*

History that would take off, in every sense of the word, with the victory of socialism. The revolution in fact meant force, although we revolutionaries would without a shadow of doubt have preferred to move forward to socialism by peaceful means. But the bourgeoisie, through its instrument of repression, the state, refused to give up its power peacefully. Force, therefore, was a necessity which it was not in our power to escape, nor could we avoid acting in accordance with its requirements.

It was true that what was happening in Lebanon was not a socialist revolution in the strict sense of the word. However, it was something close to that – a step of such enormous importance in the right direction that it could be regarded as a first step in the revolution. The part that our party, the Communist Party, was playing as the vanguard of the working class was shining proof of that.

Mr Kawabata, I am almost laughing at what I am telling you. It's almost as if I were saying it with a touch of superiority. It's as if the 'blame' fell on them, *them*, the others, as if I alone were the victim and they were the executioners. How can this be, when it is I who am naturally quick to feel guilt, sometimes without any justification?

On the subject of feeling guilt, listen:

I was once walking along a street leading to Hamra Street. A few yards in front of me someone dressed in military uniform was walking, perhaps a member of one of the many militias, or a soldier in one of the regular armies that passed through our country. In front of the 'soldier', a few yards farther on, there was a young woman walking in the company of a man. The woman was wearing a dress a little above the knee, and had pretty, fair-skinned legs. The sun hadn't had a chance yet to do its work on people's bodies, as we were still at the beginning of spring. The 'soldier' was staring steadily at the woman's legs, as was I, both because the sight was attractive in itself, but more particularly because there were only a few women who dared to wear short dresses in West Beirut during that period.

As I was walking faster than he was, I overtook the 'soldier' and found myself between him and the woman. I suddenly noticed that my presence between them was (perhaps) stopping him from seeing her legs. So I crossed the pavement and overtook the woman and the man who was with her, leaving the 'soldier' to take his enjoyment unhindered.

I thought often and for a long time about this incident later, wondering what had driven me to act as I did. It was quite certainly fear of the man in military uniform, who might have been from a faction in control in this half of the city, and who would have been furious with me – with me, who was always surprising myself in the role of hero in these situations of gallantry and chivalry! An extremely pretty woman is overtaken by a man in the street, who annoys her by looking at her in a vulgar way, and tries to touch her ... so I come up, and land him a first blow with my fist at the top of his stomach. He doubles up, and I deal him a second blow. The woman thanks me, and I acknowledge her thanks cursorarily, perhaps just with a nod of the head, without speaking. Then I go off.

If it had been peacetime, Mr Kawabata, would I have felt the desire to leave the 'soldier' to take his enjoyment of two innocent legs like this? Would I have spontaneously mounted guard on my imagination, so as not to surprise myself dreaming of twisting his body with one single blow?

So, Mr Kawabata,

Why do I seem like an innocent dragged into a forest of blood, injustice and destruction?

Is it because the Soviet Union has collapsed, and the Communist Parties have sunk below the horizon?

I can understand that a man should distance himself from an event, so as to speak about it with some neutrality, but to mock convictions which we held, or rather, I held, from the bottom of the heart... *The bottom of the heart! Another unchanging expression! How is it that language writes itself through us? How is it that we are merely its vehicles?*

We worked with these convictions to the end. To the point of murder.

Yes, to the point of murder!

Which of us did not kill with his own hand, which of us did not kill with his tongue?

Except for *him*, of course. My friend.

That was certainly why he was walking about pleased with himself, aloof, on the pavement just in front of the passage leading to the Hamra Building garage.

In this passage, which crossed the pavement, there was a ditch black with sewer water, the sewers of a Beirut that was just emerging from its impossible wars.

The stream of people on the pavement automatically avoided this ditch, so that the only people to fall into it were those who had become detached from the mainstream for some reason.

Except for him!

He, who was neither following the current of the stream, nor falling.

Because my friend knew the place.

He was walking with the stream, but with a different kind of step. His walk was slower. He was dawdling, as if his aim was simply to walk along the pavement in Hamra Street, not to reach anywhere in particular. Here he was, then, not in a hurry to reach anywhere. Places would be waiting for him, yearning for him, happy when he set foot on them.

That was after the end of the war, when the crossing points dividing the Lebanese had been opened and the armed militias been dissolved, when the dividing lines in the capital Beirut had been removed, and the dogs had slunk back to the populated quarters.

He was walking along with his head slightly in the air, looking into the distance, and holding a *misbaha* in both hands level with the top of his stomach. His bearing was upright, despite a slight paunch. His moustaches were blacker than the hair on his head, which had all turned white. A beard carefully trimmed. He was certainly just coming from the barber's at that moment.

The smartest thing about him was his suit. A grey suit, with a carefully knotted tie, and a white shirt with a collar that circled his neck without constricting it.

A suit that had only just emerged from the cleaner's, pressed for some special occasion.

And smiling!

As if nothing had happened.

He was smiling ever so gently, looking in front of him into the distance, just over the heads of everyone else, as if he were constantly afraid that the camera of history would surprise him in an unhistorical pose, and would convey to coming generations a distorted picture of him.

Was it this smile that made me so angry?

As if nothing had happened.

As if this convulsion that had lasted fifteen years – *by the way, Mr Kawabata, why did the Western media portray us as if we were some strange specimens of humanity? Why this malice, why this blindness on the part of people who defend themselves from each other with atomic bombs? How did you look at us in Japan?*

As if he were innocent of this convulsion that had lasted fifteen years. As if he had never repeated in his lectures and speeches on every possible occasion, and especially among the combatants, that 'defeat is forbidden us' and that we were 'compelled to be victorious'.

His impudence reached such a point that he would later boast, after he had resigned from his party activities, that his hands had not a single spot of blood on them. He was even active in the movement opposed to the struggle. Then he changed into a 'marginal' activist, during which time he devoted himself entirely to gambling, on the basis that everything was permitted except killing.

Gambling was a form of struggle against the war.

When I was a young man, Mr Kawabata, I saw with my own eyes that blood could bend the neck of a killer. Because blood was heavy. 'There is blood on his neck,' we used to say.

I watched a funeral procession from the roof of our house. I saw the dead man stretched out in a coffin being carried on people's shoulders. There were dark patches on his white shirt – the same number, said one of our comrades, as the holes that the bullets had made in his chest. I saw all the neighbours walking behind the corpse. I saw that one of them had a neck bent because of some weight on it, although he was actually holding his head up slightly. He was wearing exactly the same as the dead man, so much so that I thought he was his brother. Later I learned that he was his killer.

But when I saw *him* (my friend) in Hamra Street, I was surprised by the fact that his neck had not a single trace of a drop of blood on it. (I was surprised!) It was absolutely straight, as if totally innocent, sinking down and disappearing into the collar of his shirt, or emerging from it to carry his head on top, with the confidence of an upright man, and the unself-consciousness of an inanimate being.

His neck was slightly, very slightly, on the stout side, but without a single fold showing on it. Smooth as the neck of a virgin, and unblemished – the colour of children who hadn't known filth in the streets or the excrement of domestic animals.

He started boasting – this man, who was famous for saying 'defeat is forbidden us' and 'we are compelled to be victorious' – that he'd never fired a shot at anyone in a war that had killed thousands, and had injured, disfigured, paralysed, orphaned, widowed or destroyed scores of times as many.

To give his words the absolute ring of truth, he would always relate an incident that happened to him at the beginning of the war in 1975, when the President of the Republic (a Maronite) appointed a military government headed by a Sunni officer. *At that time – before the Ta'if agreement, that is, which reduced the powers of the President of the Republic in favour of the Prime Minister (a Sunni) and the Speaker of Parliament (a Shi'ite) – the powers of the President enabled him to dismiss the government and appoint a new government.* The civilian Sunni leaders had refused to head a government whose task was to take in hand the security situation (i.e. to curb Palestinian armed activity on Lebanese soil), either out of fear for their own political fate, or from conviction. The armed Palestinian presence was very popular, especially in Sunni circles, for most of the Palestinians were Sunni – to the extent that the Mufti of the Lebanese Republic once expressed the view that the Palestinians were the Muslim army in Lebanon (in the sense that the majority of the Lebanese army itself was Christian).

My friend, then, was returning to his home in the Shiyyah district, which today is part of what has become known as the southern suburbs – a district inhabited by Shi'ites who have come from the south and from the Bekaa Valley in particular.

It was evening. Shots could be heard coming from several streets that had begun to turn into permanent front lines between the two halves of the capital, Beirut.

The party's position was clear and straightforward. No to military government (the rightist media called it 'government by the military'), by any means. Including military means, that is.

Instead of going home, my friend went to the party branch headquarters close to his house. This headquarters had turned into a centre for directing armed operations. There he was given a Kalashnikov, the best-known type of personal weapon at that time, whose name was linked with wars of liberation, and whose reputation had then reached its high point because of reports coming from Vietnam of its legendary effectiveness. It could even bring down the most modern American fighter aircraft at that time, the Phantom.

He spent the night in a guardpost.

My friend always ended his account by saying that a dog attacked the guardpost, and he was uncertain what he should do. Then, out of fear, he fired on the dog and killed it. His colleagues criticized him for firing, because he had exposed the post to the risk of discovery by the enemy.

My friend continued telling the story in my presence quite brazenly, knowing that I had a detailed knowledge of the incident and its circumstances. He looked at me as he was telling it, as well as looking at the others who were hearing it for the first time.

Listen!

Listen: I confronted him once and said to him: 'Listen: I forbid you to relate this incident ever again in my presence in the way you have been telling it, with the innocence of a child! Why don't you tell how your joy turned to delight,' I said, 'when you surprised the post commander with your arrival? Tell them how he said to you that your presence among them demonstrated our party's greatness and the correctness of its line: a university professor just returned from Paris where he has been awarded a doctorate in political science, carries weapons and fights alongside simple people (they are not simple, you replied, with your well-known modesty, they are the makers of history) and spends the night with them in the trenches?! Why don't you tell them how happy and excited you were at that stage? Don't you remember what you said to me? – that we're now (i.e. at that stage) living what is written in the books: the revolutionary stage! The forces of revolution carry arms to defend their future for the sake of liberation and change!'

Didn't we compare ourselves to the Glorious October revolutionaries? Didn't we make comparisons between them and ourselves?

Lenin was personally supervising our actions, I mean our operations! He was our immediate authority. We appealed to him about absolutely everything!

We were pressurising the ruling class to abandon power so that we could take it over ourselves, as the vanguard of the revolutionary movement. Some people objected, alleging that our actions were no different from the actions of the right against whom we were fighting. A lot of killing was being done by our allies on the basis of identity cards, many robberies were taking place, and Christian interests and homes were being pillaged and destroyed in the areas where our allies the Palestinians (and ourselves with them) had begun to assume control. When anyone objected, the response to them was the passage from Lenin where he said that the revolution was bound to be infiltrated by opportunists, but that these people could not change the overall course of events!

It was also pointed out that the bourgeoisie (we Communists in particular refused to use the term 'Christians' because it wasn't a scientific term) only feared for their wealth and possessions, and that the robberies, destruction and terror that were being directed against them would scare them and force them to make concessions to us.

To us!

We Communists, the vanguard organization of the working class, peasants, revolutionary intellectuals and all honourable people, must be the tip of the spear that would cut the throat of the Lebanese bourgeoisie – with its Christian majority – and defend the Palestinian revolution so that it could continue the struggle against Israel.

Wasn't it you who confided to me some years after

the start of the war that you'd wanted to ask some questions that night, and argue, and say: 'How is it that the Palestinians are the effective force, the principal fighting force, that it is they who plunder, occupy, make gains and losses, while we are only a supporting force? And how, seeing that this is the case, are they going to present us with the victories they achieve, as a gift, so that *we* can rule?'

How?

Don't you remember how you said to me one day that the Phalange slogan – 'no state within the state' (a reference to the fact that the Palestinians had begun to create a state of their own within Lebanon) – would certainly have been valid if *we* had been the Lebanese state? Don't you remember how you told me you hadn't been able to sleep that night, as you'd been assigned the bed of a comrade of ours who'd been killed that morning, in a ground-floor room in a building where he was the watchman? That you hadn't been able to sleep in his bed spread out on the floor when he hadn't had a chance to make it? And that there were shoes beside it? Shoes of his, and clothes and other things that he had used only a few hours before, when he was alive.

Why couldn't you sleep that night?

Why did you go to our comrade who was head of station and tell him you usually stayed awake at night and didn't usually sleep until dawn, and that it was therefore better for you to stay in the observation post and keep guard? The comrade agreed, thanked you for your enthusiasm, and told you that your presence among the comrades had raised their morale greatly.

Don't you remember the ideas that came to you while you were stretched out on our martyred comrade's bed, when you smelled the smell of his sweat, of his socks, of the whole room? When you saw the dirty plates on the sink, and the tea cups? You were afraid he would come back. You couldn't sleep. You smoked and longed for a glass of whisky. It terrified you to look among his things in the room for a bottle to pour a glass from, desperate for it as you'd never been desperate for anything before! Didn't you wonder at that moment whether he'd taken his weapon and gone to the front line, after hearing you talking in a meeting called by the local party to incite a rising of the masses?

Why then did you continue to give lectures, and persist in explaining the party line, and in defending the party and its operations?

Just a flicker of bourgeois nervousness, you told me. 'It isn't easy,' you said, 'for a *petit-bourgeois* intellectual like ourselves to escape from his bourgeois class consciousness that quickly or easily.'

Your stomach turned at the sight of blood. None the less, you valued my piece highly and congratulated me on it, telling me that we were in need of precisely this sort of literature. This was revolutionary literature that told the truth in an artistic way, revealing and illuminating reality, and producing a deeper knowledge of it. This was literature committed to the interests of the masses, and to the path of history.

It raised the morale of our comrades, so that they could confront death proudly.

You said it was our duty, as revolutionary intellectuals, to raise the morale of our comrades who were sacrificing themselves. This was the least we could do for them.

You also said: 'Because fear of death might turn us into pacifists' (you used the French form *pacifiste*), 'that is, advocates of peace at any price!'

You said: 'Because fear of death would hinder the revolution...'

The thing that you most liked about my piece was the passage in which I said:

'We do not have a monopoly on martyrdom. The river draws its water from every source.

'We only claim a monopoly:

On marching firmly towards the end of this world.

'We are the end of this world.'

What you liked about these words was how I had fashioned reality with infinite precision and intelligence. And with extreme eloquence.

We, the party of the working class, it was we who possessed a scientific theory, and it was this theory that led us and guided us in our dealings with reality. Even if we made mistakes in the details (the tactics), we would not make mistakes in the essence (the strategy). Our allies, who had not adopted this revolutionary scientific theory as their guide, were continually exposed to vacillation and destruction. Hence the truth of the phrase: 'We are marching firmly towards the end of this world.'

Its importance came from its correctness, and also its beauty. The revolution was beauty, and everything that was beautiful was for the revolution.

You were amazed by the passage:

'The alphabet will no longer end with *ya*', for our martyrs will be set up as new letters.

'From today, not a word will be complete without them.'

Your delight in it sprang from the fact that it grasped one of the principal articulations of reality, namely that the revolution would bring about a radical change in social reality, and would bring us to the threshold of history. It would be a dynamic transformation, always for the better. Then again, transforming reality also meant transforming the superstructure of society, including language (even though language was naturally unlike other parts of the superstructure in some respects).

As our revolutionary theory was a scientific theory, and since it taught us that the interests of the working class, and with them the interest of the masses, coincided objectively with materialist (i.e. scientific) theory and with scientific development in all spheres – for this reason the statement: 'Without them' (i.e. our martyrs) 'science will not be complete; it is with them that science necessarily begins!' took on profound dimensions.

'I congratulate you, Rashid, you are the essence of a great writer! Carry on! I will suggest to the party that you are exempted from all other tasks except for writing. Reread comrade Brecht's *Life of Galileo* once a week:

'My thoughts multiply when I eat a tasty meal.'

Real magic was always to be found in these quotations:

'The only reality to impose itself is the reality we ourselves impose. The victory of reason is the victory of people who believe in it.'

'We have stripped the earth of its central position, and now we must empty the heaven of its masters.'

'Knowledge of the truth on the part of the masses will put an end to their entanglement with misery. When people know the truth, suppressing them becomes a difficult operation.'

'If people know the truth, it will not then be in their power to bear this subservience, misery and subjection for the sake of a heaven which no longer exists.'

'Hunger is to be unable to get anything to eat. It is not a test from God to try the patience of man.'

His eyes filled with tears when he reached the words:

*'Our martyrs have broken the limits of the alphabet, which from now has become infinite in number.'*

Then he raised his glass – we were drinking at his house – and invited all our comrades to drink a toast to the following sentence:

*'Our buds envy our flowers.'*

What I meant by this, Mr Kawabata, was that we Communists (all of us) were jealous of our comrades who had gone before us to martyrdom. We awaited our turn with patience exhausted. Buds waiting to open as martyrs!

*It was said of the Iranian Islamic fighters who came to Lebanon after the Iranian revolution that they used to greet each other with the words: 'Peace be upon you, Brother Martyr.'*

*Martyr in the sense of what he would become.*

*We went before them. But in this sense no one goes before anyone. It is the oldest honour. I know that in Japan you have a very ancient custom of redemption and self-sacrifice.*

Mr Kawabata,

On one feeble hair depends the fate of the human race! Do you not know whole groups of people who committed suicide? You certainly know more than I know. But how can one resist oppression? And how can one resist a victim who has turned into an executioner for fear that he may remain a victim?


Mr Kawabata,

We were drinking together in his house. Tears poured from his eyes and ran down his cheeks, when he read this last sentence *'Our buds envy our flowers.'* Then he repeated the words, and the eyes of everyone present

147

filled with tears, and we were seized with a violent, pagan joy mingled with a thin mist of sorrow, and a volcanic desire to take our revenge for the comrades who had gone before us to martyrdom – those who had been tortured, those who had been abducted, those whose corpses had not been identified, those who had been murdered, those who had disappeared, and those whose limbs had been amputated as a lesson.

Mr Kawabata, I lie awake with this nightmare: what if they were to return? Once again I feel the ants moving in my mouth, while my lips are sewn together like a deep wound.

What should I say to them?

And him! What would he try to convince them of? Marginality, having become one of its advocates after the long period of struggle? Democracy, political pluralism and the right of dissent – and the idea that one truth is an illusion, despite the fact that he advocated it for a time after his 'marginality period' and his release from the dirt and filth of the war? Or of Islam in the way he understood it, always with the energy for which he was known?

He was always certain of what he advocated.

When I asked him whether his conversion to Islam was out of conviction, he replied that it was not a matter of faith but of belonging. I said to him: 'Isn't it enough that you are an Arab to belong?' 'Listen,' he said, 'do you know why I bent down over my mother on her deathbed, imploring her to repeat after me the confession of faith and to become a Muslim before she died?' 'Is this intended to confirm the sincerity of your allegiance to Islam?' I replied. 'No,' he said. 'Listen. Do you know the story of Umm al-Harith ibn Abi Rabi'a? The story pained me deeply:

'It happened about one thousand, three hundred years ago according to the Muslim calendar, and was told in a book written some eleven hundred years ago. Al-Harith ibn Abdallah ibn Abi Rabi'a, the half-brother of the famous Arabian love poet 'Umar ibn Abi Rabi'a, was a generous and godfearing nobleman, and one of the leaders of the Quraysh (the Arab tribe that produced the Prophet Muhammad). The famous Umayyad caliph 'Abd al-Malik ibn Marwan once remarked of him in one of his court sessions: "By God, no mother ever had a better son than did his mother!"

'When his mother died, nobles came to her funeral. This was during the reign of the caliph 'Umar ibn al-Khattab, when the Muslim Arabs had reached the ends of the earth. Her son al-Harith heard shouting from the women who had started to wash her. When he asked what had happened, he was told that she had died a Christian, and that they had found on her neck, under her clothes, a cross which she had hidden from him.

'That story hurt me,' he said. 'I was hurt by the story of a woman who felt the need to hide her Christianity even from her son al-Harith, the fruit of her womb. Why cut oneself off like this? Why put oneself in such a difficult position? Why this revolt against the general drift, and against the climate of the age? It entails so many complexes – fear, caution, and an objective readiness to seek help from outside in case of needing to defend oneself. The minority self!'

'But this story had a happy ending,' I said, 'for Harith her son went out to the people and said: "Depart! May God have mercy on you! She has a family in religion who are more worthy of her than we or you are!" It was a popular gesture on his part, and people were pleased with what he had done.'

She was black.

My friend was silent.

Then I said to him that the Arabs had been Christians before Islam, and that they had been part of Islamic Arab civilization, and I mentioned to him some names (he knew them well) of people prominent in Arab history and Arab–Islamic history. He interrupted me. 'Be quiet!' he said. 'What does this sort of thing mean now – talking like nice people who solve problems with eloquent expressions? I am here now in the Muslim sector and I cannot move to the other sector. I don't want to anyway, especially after what's happened. I want to live, I want to marry, I want to have children. I can no longer bear to spend my time sleeping – when my luck is with me – with a 'marginal' woman who has rebelled against the norms of mankind and who has been passed from man to man. I haven't been successful in marriage so far because I cannot accept a woman who has known a man before me. How do you expect me to sleep for a lifetime with a woman on whose body I can smell the odours of men who have known her before me?

'Why haven't *you* married, Hasan?'

'I know a lot of people who haven't married for the same reason.'

'Have you ever seen the sea?' Sadiq asked me.

I knew that the sea was huge and frightening, that the oceans extended to infinity, that water comprised two-thirds of the surface of the earth, and that the oceans were deeper than the mountains were high. I knew that a tiny amount of metal would sink, while a forest of trees would float.

*I smell in this eloquence the scent of blood, Mr Kawabata.*

150

But I had not yet seen the sea with my own eyes directly.

'If the earth were round as you say, surrounded by the heavens on every side, how could water stay on it? Wouldn't it have flowed down from the top of the earth, and spilled into the heavens below?'

The heavens below.

'Then what is the earth like?' I asked him.

'How should I know? How would you know?' he replied.

*What is the earth like, Mr Kawabata?*

Mr Kawabata,

When I was hit, hit very seriously indeed, in my neck and shoulder, in every part of my being, I remained lying on the ground for a long time, bleeding. No one dared to approach me because the position was still being shelled. Meanwhile, I was hovering between life and death. I opened my eyes after my return from death as if opening them, not for the first time in my life, but for the first time in history.

I say: I was opening my eyes after returning to life, as if I was opening them for the first time in history. My gaze fell on things that were clear and bright, as if they were just emerging from the prehistoric gloom.

Mr Kawabata,

Today you know well what death is, so you are better able than anyone else to understand what I am saying: after every lapse into unconsciousness, I would open my eyes for the first time in history. Perhaps the same thing didn't happen to you, since I believe you closed your eyelids once only. And remained like that.

The film of my life didn't pass before my eyes quick

as a flash during those moments, as people say it does. This film passed by on other, more difficult occasions.

When I returned to consciousness, I was seeing for the first time in history.

Seeing, nothing else!

That repeated itself several times before the pain — pain, not death — began to shoot right through me.

Mr Kawabata,

During that period, death was what I wished for. I was not feeling pain. It was absolute rest. *It seems that this last expression might be about to run away with me!*

Death is nothingness!

Oh!

Sir, either language is not helping me, or else I can no longer master it, but my consolation is that you understand me. This is a great consolation.

It gives me great pleasure, Mr Kawabata, that you understand the difficulty — perhaps the impossibility — of a man describing a death he has experienced, a death that only lasted for a few moments, but was repeated several times in the space of a few minutes.

For a moment I was dead. I felt no pain, I could not see, I could not think, I was not worried, I was not afraid. When I returned to life, I felt a deep yearning for the preceding moment.

Sir, I want to tell you something I have never told anyone before. My friends have forgotten, especially *him*, that one day in the past I was wounded.

Indeed, when I remind any of them today that I was wounded, they seem surprised. How can I permanently impress on their consciousness that my neck is bent to the right, not naturally, but as a result of a shell. It seems as if they hear what I am saying and understand what it means, but in fact they are simply waiting to take the opportunity when a moment presents itself – it might be a breath I take to enable me to go on talking – to take the floor from me immediately and proceed to talk about their own circumstances. I wish one of them would talk about something worth paying attention to. It is pure garbage, trivial, worthless chatter, enough to make you lose any pleasure in conversation; enough to make you lose everything, like confidence for example . . .

Confidence in people, or even in the human race.

No one can put up with me for the time it takes me to express the searing pain I felt, more searing than the sorrows of summer (I cannot help being carried away by eloquence). I felt pain. So I have begun to know what pain is.

Pain, Mr Kawabata, makes death easy for you, indeed it turns it into a necessary thing, into a dream. *Who am I saying this to? To you! But, sir, if I supposed that you knew what I was telling you, I would stop speaking at once. But it is impossible to suppose that, while I am seeking your help against my countrymen.*

I am certain that if I had suffered your pain, I would have committed suicide.

Ah, Mr Kawabata, death was easy for you. How far had pain brought you? How you had suffered in every direction!

I am certain that my pain is only a fraction of what you yourself suffered, but I too have suffered pain. Please listen:

I hear everyone saying: 'I'm fighting sleep,' meaning that he is struggling to keep his eyes open to stay awake.

Except me!

I prepare myself and get ready for it, for hours every day.

Before it comes – a long time before it comes – I

retreat into myself, to prepare myself and open my pores for it. I begin waiting for it to come. After I have exhausted myself, it comes. Sometimes I have stopped taking notice before it comes.

He is my king and master, and I am his kingdom, his beautiful, chosen child-bride.

When he penetrates me, it is through every pore of my body, like water seeping into sand. I have never felt myself a woman – I, who am so jealous of my masculinity – except with him. He is my master, taking me whenever he wants, at any moment of the long night he wishes. I open myself to him wide, keeping on me the smells of the day if I am expecting him to crave strong smells – the remains of food between my teeth, the dandruff in my hair, the dirt between my toes, under my nails and armpits. Sometimes I wash, for the taste of the lover changes.

No wife ever waited for a lover as I have awaited him, no young girl, or mother, or shepherdess or land. *I smell the scent of blood in the eloquent style of these phrases!*

Listen:

I once wanted to write the story of a man whose stomach had been removed by the doctors, who kept him alive on serum for some reason, for what they'd intended to be a few hours. The man was able to live by smell alone for a few weeks after that, but in the end he died. He died for all sorts of reasons except his stomach!

I say 'for all sorts of reasons', Mr Kawabata, for how much you have suffered in every direction.


'Whether the earth revolves or does not revolve, my son,' said my mother, 'is all the same to you. Either way, you have to study to get your diploma to be able to get a job. What does it matter to you whether or not Sadiq is convinced?'

'Mother,' I replied, 'it matters a lot to me that people know the truths revealed by science and act in accordance with them. This is a vital matter. Our society will not be able to pick itself up after a fall otherwise.' *Picking oneself up, with us, is often after a fall.*

My mother was silent when I spoke to her like this. She would wait for me to finish what I wanted to say, then repeat that I had to get a diploma so that God could give me a job that would protect me against poverty, and the hardships of the world, and its unpredictable temperament.

When my neighbour died, I went to the village to attend the funeral and to mourn him. I repeated a phrase that I had read in a classical Arabic book:

'Can you still face the facts?'

But what is the universe like, Mr Kawabata?

Nothing!

Nothing, I assure you!

That is what I experienced when I died. During my death. When I died for a few moments that were repeated several times in a few minutes. I would open my eyes after being brought to life again, and I would see for the first time in history. Only two people understand what I am saying: you, because you have died, and I, because my death has been repeated several times!

My friends have forgotten that I was ever wounded, so how are they to believe that I have experienced death?

I still remember it as if it was now: I would open my eyes and see. Nothing else. Nothing beautiful, nothing ugly. Nothing distant, nothing near.

For the first time only. Without any astonishment.

Without any feeling of surprise. So I began to understand the camera. For a moment I was a camera. It sees, nothing else.

Always for the first time.

I began to understand that man might be something without grief.

Before I was injured, I used to think that the whole world would be disturbed if anything bad happened to me. *Perhaps because I sometimes used to see uproar when a man fell wounded: car horns, ambulances, firing into the air or over people's heads to clear a path*. I felt regret (*I almost said 'deep regret'*) whenever I read in a newspaper that somebody's corpse had been found and that its identity was unknown.

That was all fantasy!

Mr Kawabata,

I used to think that the rhythm of the earth's rotation would be upset if I was wounded or died! It was as if I was certain that the whole universe needed me, needed my presence, to preserve its own equilibrium – in other words, that the end of the war in Lebanon would be the least important of the results of my being wounded.

The fighting continued while I lay on the ground, unable to get up. I was consumed by pain, as my blood poured out. *I believe that the Japanese also like this expression 'blood pouring out', every bit as much as we Arabs, especially when the loss of blood is for the cause*.

As I lay on the ground, voices came to me from secure positions, asking my name!

As if their knowing my name would be reflected in my recovery! Like when the electricity is suddenly cut off while you are in a lift. You shout, and a voice comes from outside: 'Who is it?'

As if it was your name that would save you.

Exactly!

With us Arabs – and I do not think we are alone in this – your name can save you or destroy you.

Listen:

The Muslims circumcise their children. That is one of their religious obligations. Christians are not compelled to circumcise their children, and generally do not do so except for medical reasons. Like most Christians, I have not been circumcised, nor has anyone suggested that I should be.

What I am saying to you is a prelude to the following incident.

We were fleeing from Beirut in a taxi. Five passengers and the driver. None of us knew any of the others. The only thing bringing us together was that we were in a single taxi on an endless road – endless, not because it was long, but because of the many dangers that might happen on it. At a certain moment on the road, the driver stopped for us to rest a little. We all went to relieve ourselves. It was open country, with no trees and no rocks.

In circumstances like these, modesty demands privacy. But on this occasion, the fear that one of us might 'uncover' another, was even stronger than modesty. So we went a long way apart.

A very long way.

Each of us knew why he was moving away. And why the others were moving away.

I don't remember the faces of anyone in the taxi. That is not because my memory has let me down – you know now how prodigious my memory is – but because I hadn't looked at anyone's face, nor had anyone looked at my face. None of our eyes had met. Not even once. I had heard none of their voices, and no one had heard mine. The weather was cold, the taxi windows were shut, and we were all covering as much of our bodies as possible in winter clothes.

Mr Kawabata,

Among us, places are defined by the similarity of names. This is how one should define the war according to the professors!

Among us, wars happen in order that the names in one place should be alike.

In our country, your name defines you, and your father, and your grandfather's grandfather, and the place where you live. If your own name doesn't help, then your father's name will help. Or else the place where he is buried. *I hope you don't need any clarification: things are presumably like that in your country too, and in other countries:*

*Jean, Jacques, Jean-Jacques, Jean, Charles, Jean-Charles . . .*

It will help you to escape if you're unable to reveal your name in this sort of situation, for the person trying to find out your name will take you to hospital in case you are one of them, and sometimes a man will be tempted to act with no particular motive – 'for God's sake', as we Arabs say. Incidentally, Mr Kawabata, this is a characteristic of mine that I rather like. I don't know whether it goes back to my being an Arab, but whatever the reason, the idea of performing a service for no reward appeals to me – a service no one knows about, even those most affected by it. I am naturally not claiming that this is my constant main preoccupation. But it is certainly a constant dream of mine, one of those many dreams that I surprise myself taking refuge in unconsciously.

It sometimes happens, for example, that I spend a whole day living just on water, with no food, when I've seen the picture of a man dying from hunger somewhere in the world. When Israel expelled four hundred Palestinians from their homes, and flung them into the open air in Lebanon, I opened my bedroom window that night and, despite the intense cold, slept on my bed in my clothes without any blankets, so as to share the Palestinian refugees' suffering in my own way.

Perhaps you don't know, Mr Kawabata, what I am talking about. Many things have happened since you passed away. But you doubtless know that a state called Israel was established on Palestinian land, which involved the expulsion of a large proportion of the original Palestinian Arab inhabitants, and also led to much bloodshed. I am not reminding you of this out of nostalgia or hatred, because I now believe that we must approach the world another way. And this is impossible.

I am reminding you of it to tell you that I suffer twice when the victim becomes an executioner.

Why is the victim always an executioner, Mr Kawabata?

I sometimes say: it is my good fortune to have been born an Arab.

Perhaps you will find no meaning in this statement. But you will certainly not go so far as to regard it as chauvinism. I am not a chauvinist at all, you can be absolutely certain of that. I simply love the fact that I was born an Arab. I love the light in my country, and I hate the cold.

In Agatha Christie's novel *Death on the Nile*, a lady says that she hates two things above all: heat and wickedness.

For myself, I hate the cold quite openly, and prefer heat a thousand times. This is not a defect either on her part or on mine, and neither of us intends any offence. We have agreed on that in advance, and there is no need for us to argue about it.

*By the way*, the crime that took place on that tourist boat on the Nile was nothing to do with the Egyptians (who are Arabs, like the Lebanese). Nothing whatever, either directly or indirectly. They were simply onlookers. I don't say this to make you think that I am one of those people who dream of recovering Andalucia for the Arabs, like many of my fellow countrymen, especially our poets, writers and intellectuals. It won't change your opinion of me if I make fun of these dreams, when I've already told you that I suffer twice when the victim becomes an executioner, but I am certain...

*I am certain?*

that we might be saved – humanity, that is – if we approached things from another angle. This is impossible. I am a Maronite who loves goat's yoghurt, I love it, but not to spite anyone else. It is just that if left to my own inclinations (*to my own inclinations!*) I would choose goat's yoghurt rather than any other sort of yoghurt.

Do you know how I got the idea of writing about the man who didn't die though his stomach had been removed? The idea came to me when I realized that man would not be saved unless he could live without food! Don't you agree with me that eating is an indescribably violent activity? We chew with our teeth in order to change things into ourselves. With our teeth we change what is different from us into 'us'.

Don't you think that fasting, in many religions and in some philosophical schools, is simply the human expression of a rejection of the 'animal' that is in us, and a deep desire to be free of this innate violence?

Do you suppose that is why some doctors prescribe the drinking of wine in moderation, on the basis that wine is the most ethereal of substances? *Wine in Islam is the drink of the people of Paradise, while in Christianity during the Divine Mass, it is a symbol of the blood of Christ, no, the blood of Christ itself.*

Among us Arabs, abstaining from food or eating only a little of it suggests a commendable restraint.

Jahiz, the famous Arab writer who died in the second half of the ninth century, says, in the *Book of the Crown* attributed to him:

*It is a king's right to expect his guest not to abandon his manners, and not to follow his natural inclinations, for example by exhibiting excessive greed or seeking to sate his hunger.*

Even kings, Mr Kawabata, are afraid of this 'animal' that chews and turns what is different into what is like (with all that that entails!).

And the masses, Mr Kawabata? The angry masses? The roar of the masses? If you heard the roar of the masses from somewhere, you would think it the roar of all the ocean waves together. A roar coming from the abysses and caves of eternity.

But goat's yoghurt to my mind has a pure taste! (*Unless the goats are grazed on poisoned grass, in which case their milk can become the source of a malignant fever.*) Have you ever tasted their milk heated with a little mint from a garden warmed by the sun in front of the door, and watered from a nearby spring, water from a spring that is cool even in the heat of summer?

I used to feel, and I still do feel, when I drink goat's milk that I am at peace with life. I feel a sort of joy. I love the sea, and am beguiled by its secrets, and love the desert, and am beguiled by its secrets. I love all the trees of the earth, and I love every sort of plant.

Mr Kawabata, so far when I have talked to you of the accident that happened to me, I have got no further in my story than the first few moments. Those moments that spanned only a brief interval, after which everything returned to normal. *Everything returned, returns to normal! It is as if someone penned this expression on my behalf – there is a smell of blood in the air.*

In the hospital, women cried for me. I didn't see them, I only heard their voices weeping over me. I imagined myself at home with my family, stretched out on the bed in the middle of the living room, surrounded by my mother and sisters, female relatives and neighbours. I was happy, because the dead feel no pain.

Later, I found out that the women weren't crying for me, but for some other passers-by like myself who had been killed in the same explosion. We'd all been taken away together in a single vehicle and put into a single room, I don't remember why.

In the vehicle, they laid someone on top of me, which stopped me breathing. I thought that he was stopping me breathing on purpose, so that I would die. He was killing me, and I desperately wanted to push him off me. His head was on my shoulder, with his mouth over the gaping wound in my neck, as if he were kissing me or staunching the flow of my blood with his lips and tongue.

In fact, it was a corpse. *In fact!*

I found out later that the women were not my family. That was why they were crying. They were looking at me with murderous looks of jealousy and envy. I had escaped, and their son had been killed. There was nothing about me to suggest that I was a citizen necessary for the stability of the earth, so they wanted to substitute me for their son in the coffin that had arrived, with others, in numbers to match the corpses – so I believed, and so logic dictated that I should believe.

*Can you imagine, Mr Kawabata, how things might turn out, if one man could die in place of another?*

It seems that their son was dear to their hearts, indescribably dear.

Then I realized that the number of coffins that had been brought to the room exceeded the number of corpses around me by one.

I could not work out why! Had they thought me dead by mistake, and so brought a coffin for me? Or had the dear victim's family deliberately played a trick to put me in the coffin?

I was alone with the dead, in this dark room. Meanwhile, people were coming in and going out, after looking at our faces by the light of a small handlamp. I was losing and regaining consciousness.

Some time after I remember being brought into the room, I was able to ask one of the people coming in and going out if my injury was serious and whether I would die. I didn't hear a reply. But I did hear a voice say on one occasion – I think it was a woman's voice – 'My beloved has passed away! So let those that will die now die!'

After a while there was no one left in the room except myself, alone with a single coffin placed near the door in front of me. Then some people came. I couldn't distinguish their features in the gloom, I couldn't hear their voices. With a movement that seemed as if they had agreed on its finest details in advance, they carried me in the direction of the coffin.

Were they going to put me into it?

I no longer remember – because of my repeated lapses into unconsciousness – whether I told them that I was still alive, and that it was wrong for them to put me in the coffin, to shut the lid, and to bury me when

I had not yet died. I began to strike the lid of the coffin with my hands and feet. Rain poured from the heavens, and water trickled over me – water that in the absolute darkness seemed muddy from the earth that covered my grave. Then I heard shouting coming closer, then I heard an insistent banging of hands on the door of the tomb, then I made out the voices of my mother and sisters calling me to wake up, and I distinguished the voice of the young girl I secretly loved when I was still a young boy but didn't dare tell of my love. She was pleading with me to get up, saying that she knew of my love for her, and that she dreamed of the moment when I would reveal to her this love that had stayed buried. She told me that her marriage was a sham and her children were a joke, but that she was still the same, asking her family for permission to go out for a walk in the early evening, and promising them never to be late. And my father...

My father whose voice I hadn't heard was behind the women crying from some place deep inside him, far and distant. He was crying out of sorrow, a sorrow that shook him, covering his mouth with his hand so that his sobbing wouldn't reach me. He was bent double from a terrible pain in his abdomen.

My father was burning with a wish to know what had happened to me, and how, and who.

Grief is a very savage emotion, Mr Kawabata. To die with grief like that is more difficult than death alone.

You know that with us Arabs, there is no one who does not have a family to grieve for him. As an Arab, I have a family who may multiply at need and become a tribe, or something even more numerous and powerful, My father couldn't imagine that I would dare to withhold my name, whatever the circumstances.

Had I told them my name, Mr Kawabata, or had they guessed it, or read it after finding my identity card?

*Name, revealer of one's true identity!*

Or had they enticed me while I was unawares, tricked me and fathomed my thoughts, to discover who I was among them?

Treacherous enemy!

Then his voice surprised me, *his* voice, in the distance. What had he come to do in the middle of a family visiting the grave of their son?

*After I had passed him, Mr Kawabata, on the Hamra Street pavement, I couldn't stop myself looking back. I saw the ripped turn-up of one of his trouser legs covering the heel of his shoe, being dragged along the dirt of the pavement.*

Then his voice drew nearer, so that I could hear it clearly. Then he said, addressing me directly: 'Well done! You have been wounded and escaped, so now you can boast about your rich experience of life!'

Then I heard my mother's voice again saying, as she beat insistently on the lid of the coffin: 'How will your mother comfort you, when her eyes search for things in the light as if they were searching in a blind gloom? They no longer have any focus to attract them, and they seem to be searching in a void!'

Your mother uses both hands to get up from her chair, she pulls with them on her knees to help her lift her body, for the days are moving on in their fearful course, the body is becoming tired and illness comes close to death. The passing pain you felt, is what she suffers today without its passing. *Sadiq, this is exactly what you also said!*

*When I went in to take a last look at Sadiq before his corpse was carried away, I was troubled! I was frightened to confront him! For a long time I'd no longer seen him. This was the first time I had looked at him properly since the death of my father.*

I would secretly have liked, Mr Kawabata, to have been able to die in place of their dear relative and be forgiven, but it was an impossible thing. It is not I who made the rules, and it is not I who have ordained that waters should flow in their channels or overflow.

As for what we Arabs call in our language 'the customary way of life', it is not I who have prescribed it.

PS I hope that you may be able to spare the time to reply.